HEADLESS

Scott Cole

Grindhouse Press
PO BOX 540
Yellow Springs, Ohio 45387

Grindhouse Press #100
ISBN-13: 978-1-957504-15-5

Other Titles by Scott Cole

SuperGhost
Slices: Tales of Bizarro and Absurdist Horror
Triple Axe
Crazytimes
Departures

ONE

LINZY'S HEAD THROBBED. IT HADN'T been this bad in a while. But the heat had been brutal lately, and she always felt like garbage in the summer, so she wasn't surprised. The air conditioner in the window chugged along, trying to keep up even after the sun had descended, but it could only do so much. It was probably time to invest in a newer model, Linzy thought. This one was at least a decade old. No, more like two. Did air conditioners go bad? Seemed like a possibility, but she didn't know for sure. Either way, she could probably use one with more BTUs or whatever.

She had gotten some notification on her phone a week or two ago—something about it being the hottest month ever recorded worldwide, even in the parts of the world where it was supposed to be cold. That kind of blew her mind for a minute, but there was nothing she could do about it, so she promptly let the knowledge slip away until now.

It had rained late that afternoon, which had cooled things down a bit, but not enough, and only temporarily. As soon as the storm had stopped, the heat made sure its dominance was known again.

Her headache—the way it was focused around her eyes and

cheeks—probably meant it was going to rain again soon. Maybe overnight, maybe in the morning. She had never been so sensitive to such things, but that had changed in recent years. Sinus pain told her it was going to rain, while aching knees were a precursor to snow in the winter. She hated this stuff, hated that she was getting older. And she wasn't even old. She just wasn't twenty-five anymore. Thirty-nine was a whole other stage of life, and she wasn't thrilled about certain aspects of it.

She tried to ignore the headache. She had taken a couple Advil, which helped dull the pain some. And lying in bed in the dark helped some more. But these remedies only did so much. She should probably talk to a doctor. Maybe there was something wrong with her sinuses. Great, something else to worry about as she approached forty. Fantastic.

For the moment, she simply wanted to put the headache out of her mind. If only the pain wasn't literally front and center of where her mind sat. Of course, if she could only stop thinking such thoughts, perhaps she would be able to drift away to sleep.

She tossed, repositioning herself face-down on the opposite side of the bed—Ron's side—placing her head on the cooler of the two pillows. The sheet got twisted in the process and she had to adjust it. As hot and uncomfortable as she felt, she still needed some kind of covering. No blankets or anything like that. Just a sheet. A thin one.

She felt better on the other side of the bed. Until a moment later, when a sudden itch struck her left Achilles, after which she had to pull her hair off her neck and rearrange herself again.

Ron would be home soon, she figured. If she was still awake by the time he got in, and if he wasn't too smashed from his night out drinking with the boys, maybe she'd try to see if he could distract her from the pain for a while. A roll in the proverbial hay was always good for soothing whatever ailed her, she had discovered long ago. Insomnia? Depression? Work stress? Sex could fix it all, at least temporarily. "Not tonight, honey, I have a headache" was a sentence she had never even thought to utter her entire adult life.

She rolled over again, this time staying on the same side of the mattress but lying on her back instead. After a few more moments, she realized her eyes were wide open, staring at the ceiling fan she could barely see in the darkness, spinning almost imperceptibly over the foot of the bed.

It was hopeless. She couldn't get to sleep.

Linzy buried her chin into her chest, angling for a glance at the clock across the room. It was 12:42 a.m. Even the green LED display hurt her eyes, her headache feeling like someone squeezing her eyeballs with vise grips.

Shit, almost one a.m.? Maybe she should get up. That's what you were supposed to do, right? Get out of bed, go to a different room, maybe read a book—as long as it's a paper book. No screens.

Where the hell was Ron? Linzy hadn't realized it was quite so late. Normally, on these Boys' Nights, he'd be home by 11:30, maybe midnight at the latest. She wondered what was keeping him.

Shit, she thought again. Had she locked the door to the apartment? Little things like that were slipping her mind lately. Was this an age-related thing too? *Was she going senile?*

She questioned herself a lot these days.

No, Linzy, don't be so neurotic. You're fine. These headaches and the heat are just making you crazy. Plus, the lobby of their building had a key card system and a twenty-four-hour security guard. No one who didn't live there was getting in without a resident escort, and each person she had met in the building was nicer than the last.

She had never been able to figure out why the building didn't have central air though.

She had only lived there a few months. It had been Ron's place before, but realizing the path they were on together, they decided there was no sense in spending money on rent for two different apartments. They had started talking about buying a house, maybe even getting married. Time would tell.

Linzy stretched her body beneath the thin cotton sheet. The room was feeling a bit better now. Cooler. She hugged her midsection and caressed her sides for a second. It felt nice. The well-worn David Bowie concert t-shirt she wore to bed slid against her skin like butter. She moved her hands lower next, caressing the outer edges of her hips and then the creases of her upper thighs.

Ron had to be home soon. Maybe she'd prime herself for him and be ready to jump his bones the moment he crawled into bed beside her. She got wet instantly, just thinking about what she was planning to do. She slipped a finger under the waistband of her panties and teased the skin beneath, softly touching her smooth pubic mound. She reached her other hand below and slid her underwear off and down to her ankles, then she kicked them and the part of the sheet covering her to the foot of the bed.

Suddenly, there was a sound. Even through the hum of the air conditioner, she could hear a dull, metallic noise beyond the bedroom. The rattling of the doorknob. It sounded like it had been touched, but not turned all the way. She didn't hear the key slide into the lock either. She froze, listening over the AC and the soft whoosh of the ceiling fan.

A moment later, the door opened. Damn, she *had* forgotten to lock it, hadn't she? Hopefully Ron wasn't pissed. Hopefully he wasn't piss-drunk either. She needed something of his in proper working order.

Hopefully it *was* Ron.

She panicked for a moment, a handful of possibilities running through her mind. Thankfully they were only on the second floor. If there was some sort of emergency, she could always jump from the other window—the one the air conditioner wasn't in. The awning below would be enough to break her fall if it came to that. She had given this idea some thought before, but it had never seemed quite so real as it did now.

There were fire stairs down the hall, but they didn't do much good if you were trapped in the bedroom.

She heard Ron's feet shuffle through the apartment. Something slumped to the floor. His messenger bag? Then there was movement again. It was him. She was sure of it. She continued listening, tried to visualize what he was doing and what his level of sobriety was. She hadn't yet alerted him to the fact that she was awake.

His footsteps sounded slow. Sluggish. *Ffsssh, ffsssh.*

Thump. Did he just bump into a wall?

"Ron? I'm up, hon'," Linzy finally called out, not too loud. "Turn on a light if you can't see well enough."

He paused his movements but didn't respond. He must be drunk, Linzy thought. She rolled her eyes in the darkness but wasn't too concerned. He'd be in soon enough.

She heard some further stumbling in the dark of the living room, but eventually Ron dragged himself toward the bedroom. *Ffsssh, ffsssh, ffsssh, ffsssh.*

He bumped a shoulder into the door frame, pressing the door itself slightly more open.

"Hey babe," Linzy said. "You okay?"

Ron didn't say a word.

"Little too much to drink, huh? Well, get in bed." Her voice changed from caring to seductive. "*I've been waiting for you.*"

He took a step forward, then two, until his thighs were pressed against the side of the mattress. He stopped there. Linzy rolled in his direction and reached for him, barely able to make out the slightest hint of his silhouette. She placed a hand on his hip and squeezed. An unusual odor wafted into the room with him, which she assumed was the result of whatever he had been drinking all night. It wasn't foul, just strange, and she put it out of her mind instantly.

"You're home a little later than I expected. Hope you weren't out whoring around." Linzy chuckled, flirty, but again there was no response from Ron. Was he so blitzed he couldn't even form words? Or was he just tired? Maybe he was just fucking with her. He did that sometimes for a laugh. He had an odd sense of humor.

She decided to test the situation, sliding her hand forward to the front of his pants, where she caressed his bulge for a second.

She found his belt buckle in the dark and managed to undo it with one hand. Then she slid forward a bit more and rolled onto her stomach, kicking the rest of the sheet aside. She was perpendicular now to the way she had been lying, and face-to-face with Ron's pelvis. She used both hands to undo the button to his pants and slide the zipper down.

"Let's get you out of these, shall we?"

Ron teetered a bit as Linzy pulled his waistband outward and slid his pants and underwear together down his thighs, slowly, before letting them drop the rest of the way to the floor. Propped up on her elbows, she inched forward again and felt his body tense as she began swirling her tongue around the head of his penis. She opened wide and took all of him into her mouth next, her expert movements causing him to swell instantly atop her tongue.

Good, she thought. Not *too* drunk.

She didn't mind that he hadn't said anything. Truthfully, it was kind of hot, the moment reminding her vaguely of some fairly anonymous intimate encounters she'd had in her twenties. Men she had met in bars. Men who weren't right for her but were certainly right for the moment. Suddenly, she didn't feel her age.

She moaned as he filled her mouth entirely, and she continued to move her neck like a piston, sliding up and down his shaft, going a fraction deeper with each thrust. One of her hands had returned to his bare hip, her fingertips curled partway around his butt cheek, which she squeezed periodically. She spent a moment rubbing the underside of his balls with her other hand, then moved it up to stroke him as she focused her tongue and lips on his glans again. He was rock hard now but remained silent as she worked her magic.

She felt a hand touch the back of her head lightly, almost as if by accident. Fingertips grazed one of her shoulder blades next. She took this as a cue and pulled away from him, slurping her lips off the tip of his dick as she moved back onto her knees. Ron swiped softly in her direction as she crossed her arms in front of her body and pulled the t-shirt off over her head. Then she rolled onto one hip and lay back down on the bed, sensing Ron reach for her again.

"Mmm, strong silent type tonight, huh?" she said. "Come on, babe, *I need you to fuck me right now.*" She lay back and touched herself briefly between her legs. She was soaked. Beyond ready.

Ron patted the bed, seemingly unsure in the dark. Very little street light managed to creep in through the blackout curtains. Linzy reached out and grabbed his forearm to help guide him, and he propped a knee on the mattress and hoisted himself up. Unsteady, however, he fell sideways and collapsed beside her.

"That's okay," Linzy said with a smile, sitting back up. "I'm more than happy to take charge." She made sure he was positioned on his back, then she threw one of her legs over his hips and got into position. She grabbed his cock and stroked it gently a few times, then pressed it against her vulva. She rocked her pelvis against him, rubbing her labia up and down the underside of his hard-on, then deftly inserted him into her vagina. She slid down onto him slowly and moaned softly, but she was so wet, there was nothing to be hesitant about. Up and down she moved, slowly at first, then picking up speed quickly. It seemed they were both ready to pop and both desperately in need of sleep, so she didn't imagine it was going to be a terribly long-lasting session.

She breathed heavy, loving the way he filled her, loving the way they moved together. It was exactly what she needed. She liked being on top too, in control of the rhythm. She leaned forward and felt for Ron's arms so she could grab his wrists and hold him down in mock-restraint. He was grasping the fitted sheet, she found, which was a good sign. He was obviously enjoying the moment too. But she ripped his arms up from it and redirected them toward the headboard, where she pinned them down against the pillow, just above his shoulders.

She continued rocking against him, feeling his erection slide against her insides, and realized they hadn't yet kissed. She leaned further forward and felt her nipples graze his chest. She liked the feeling, so she stayed there for a minute, then she pulled his hands up again and led them to her breasts. He squeezed them tightly as she moved her own hands onto his ribs.

"Babe, you didn't take off your shirt?" she said between breaths. That was unusual. But, as was par for the course this night, Ron didn't say a word.

He tried to lean up toward her, but she pressed him back down to the mattress.

Her hands crept up beneath the bottom edge of his shirt, where she felt the wisp of hair on his stomach. His belly was soft, but not too big, just the way she liked it. She began undoing the buttons from the bottom of his shirt next, not that that was what she wanted to focus on. But she did want to touch the hair on his chest and press her palms against his pecs. She already felt the rumblings of an orgasm starting within, and in a moment, she wanted to be skin-to-skin with him, the coarse hair of his torso rubbing roughly against her breasts as she came.

In the process, she felt something else. Something even weirder than the fact he was wearing a shirt at all. The shirt was wet. What was up with that? Was it really still *that* hot outside, this late at night? Had he sweat through it? Or, perhaps more likely, had he spilled the last of his final drink down the front of himself?

She reached up for the next button and found the fabric to be even slicker. Her rhythm slowed as she patted his ribs and chest, the reverberations of her impending orgasm already beginning to fade away.

His shirt was soaked. And, somehow, it felt . . . *sticky?*

"Ron, what is this?" she asked, her tone suddenly far less playful than it had been since he had gotten home. "What's on your shirt?"

Once again Ron failed to respond.

"Will you please say something?!" She smacked his sternum in frustration and knocked his arms away from where they had been. His hands detached from her breasts and fell to the mattress, then he reached back up immediately and began pawing at her hips.

But she'd had enough of his silence. It had been fun at first. A turn-on, sure. But enough was enough. She wanted to know why he had come home so late and why he was soaked through his shirt. What had he been up to? *And why the fuck wasn't he talking?*

HEADLESS

The room smelled of sex but also something else. Something . . . *metallic?*

Linzy slid off him as quickly as she could without hurting herself. When she did, his hard-on smacked wetly against his paunch. She tried to dismount next, but he was still grabbing at her, making it difficult.

"Stop!" she said forcefully. It was late and she didn't want to yell, but if he kept swiping at her this way and not saying a word, she was going to get angry, and loud. A moment later, she had managed to free herself from his clutches, and she slid over to and then off her side of the bed.

She fumbled in the dark and found her t-shirt. Then she remembered how she'd slid her panties off earlier. Reaching beneath the tangled top sheet, she found them fairly easily and pulled them on.

"I don't know what your problem is," she said, frustrated, as she moved across the room in the dark, gliding along the foot of the bed without bumping it. She could see the vague silhouette of Ron's arms reaching up and outward, waving about like some maniac. What was going on with him?

Then she reached the doorway and placed a hand on the light switch. When she flipped it, she saw exactly what the problem was.

He had no head.

TWO

CARTER COULDN'T SLEEP. OR, RATHER, he couldn't *stay* asleep.

It was a strange thing, but almost from the day he turned thirty-five the previous March, he no longer seemed to be the night owl he once was. He often found himself unable to stay awake beyond ten o'clock at night, his eyelids unwilling to cooperate with his desire to watch a movie or argue with someone online. And so, rather than find himself waking up on the couch hours later with either the TV or his laptop screen watching *him*, he chose to will his body, however sluggishly, into his bedroom, where he always fell deeply asleep within moments.

The problem was staying asleep. Particularly this summer. More often than not, a few hours after crawling into bed, he would wake up, his body alerting him to the need to piss. And as soon as that seal had been broken, he was wide awake, as if he had gotten eight hours of solid rest instead of three.

He often paid for it the following afternoon, but thankfully he worked remotely and set his own schedule. Provided he accomplished his docket of tasks by the end of each week, no one at the office cared about when exactly it all got done. So whenever he needed to, he simply took a nap.

This wasn't the case every day. Not by a long shot. But what struck him as odder still was the fact that even if he did take an afternoon siesta, he always found himself unable to stay up past ten at night. Sometimes even 9:30.

He wondered if the weather had anything to do with it. He kept his apartment nice and chilly to try to combat the heat, but he was pretty sure that wouldn't affect whatever the humidity did to people. *Or would it?* He didn't know much about these things. Regardless, keeping the AC going all summer meant his electricity bill had skyrocketed the last few months. It was worth it though.

If only he could figure out the key to getting more than a few hours of sleep at a time.

He had woken up, once again, around 12:30. As usual, he popped out of bed and zombie-walked his way to the bathroom. But as soon as he began urinating, his body decided his sleepy time was up, and that was that. Just as he did most nights, he tried tricking himself into disbelief, and shuffled back to the bed, where he got under the covers and desperately tried to slip back into unconsciousness. But it rarely worked, and tonight was no exception. He lay there for twenty minutes, tossing from one side of the bed to the next, curling up nice and comfy beneath the covers, attempting desperately to will himself back to sleep. He tried thinking calming thoughts. He tensed and released every muscle. He tried breathing exercises. But none of it worked. After thirty or forty minutes, he finally decided to give in and get up.

He considered putting something on the TV but couldn't think of anything he was in the mood to watch. And he definitely didn't feel like trawling the depths of social media. As exhausting as that experience had become, it wasn't something that would help him get back to sleep. Ten minutes later, though, he was online, the glow of his laptop illuminating the room as a notification from an old message board he'd been following for years alerted him to the fact that several new Aphex Twin tracks had been dumped to SoundCloud for free, without any warning, as usual. He knew he better download them before they disappeared.

Most of what he listened to these days was electronic music, nearly all of it instrumental, and for whatever reason mostly from artists who had gotten their start in the '90s. He had grown up mostly listening to metal, and some punk, but he eventually found that certain electronic musicians' stuff was way more aligned with his taste, and in some cases, he found it to be far heavier and more pleasantly challenging to listen to than the guitar sounds of his youth. Some of it was just really beautiful sounding and melodic. He liked that stuff too.

Outside his door, there was a thump in the hallway. That was nothing out of the ordinary, even for this time of night. People worked and played at all different hours, and part of living in an apartment building was learning to live with—or at least among—other people. Strangers. Strangers who maybe came home with new prospective hookups or who maybe worked jobs with unusual shifts or who maybe woke up in the middle of the night and puttered around trying to find something to occupy their time with because sleep itself was but a distant dream.

Another thump came a moment later. Then another, even louder. Something was going on. He heard footsteps. And a woman's voice? What was she saying?

"Help . . ."

Carter set his laptop on the coffee table in front of the couch and jogged lightly across the living room toward his front door. He wasn't entirely sure he had heard any of the commotion right. It was the middle of the night after all. Somebody came stumbling down the hall at least a couple times a week, spewing some sort of nonsense or trying to cause some chaos for their less-inebriated friends. That was typically something that happened on weekend nights, but nothing would be terribly surprising, even if it was Tuesday night. Or, technically, Wednesday morning.

"Please . . ." Another thump, this time right outside his door. And was that crying? "Somebody help . . ."

Carter reached the door, unsure whether or not to open it right away. He wanted to assess the situation before getting involved. He placed his hands on either side of the frame and leaned in toward the peephole. But all he could see were the plain wall directly across from his door and the curved contours of the distorted hallway in its magnified form. At the edges of his circular view, he could see a couple of his neighbors' doors, but they were closed and unremarkable.

Then he noticed the tiny dark smear on the wall, about chest level.

"Help . . ."

Not knowing what he might find, Carter made the decision to slide the chain off his door and undo the deadbolt as quietly as possible. He paused a moment, then turned the knob as gently as he could before cracking the door open, ready to slam it shut again if danger suddenly presented itself.

He saw nothing down the hall to the right, but he was able to get a better look at the smear on the wall directly across from his door. There wasn't much to it—just a few faint lines, as if someone had touched the wall with a mostly dry paintbrush. But the mark was red, which was concerning.

Before he could open the door any further, he heard another thump, and he heard the voice again. A woman. She was sobbing.

Carter stepped into the hall and spotted her to the left, several doors down. She was petite, cute, with shoulder-length dark hair, and wearing a long t-shirt. There might have been shorts underneath but he couldn't tell.

"Hi. Are you . . . *okay?*" Carter said, the words stumbling out as if he had never spoken them before.

The woman turned around, her eyes frantic and tearing. Her hands shook. Her knees wobbled. She held her arms away from her body. And that's when Carter noticed the red smears on her right elbow and forearm.

"Help," she said again, this time even softer than her earlier pleas had been. She hesitated for a second with her movement, then she ran straight to Carter, who ushered her into his apartment before shutting the door as quickly as he could without slamming it and throwing the locks.

THREE

LINZY WAS SHAKING SO MUCH, she had trouble washing all the blood off her arm. In the mirror, she could see specks of it dried reddish-brown on her face, and a big still-wet spot on the side of Bowie's face on her t-shirt too. Some had dripped onto her leg as well, but she didn't know if Ron had tried to grab her there or if the gore had just dripped off her arm.

It probably made sense to just take a shower.

She opened the bathroom door.

"I'm on hold with 911, if you can believe that," Carter said. He was sitting on the couch, forward on the cushion, on the far side of the living room. As if on cue, sirens sounded in the distance. "Busy night, I guess."

This apartment had a totally different layout than her own, Linzy noticed, and it was sparsely decorated in the way bachelor apartments tended to be, at least in her experience. Standard-issue white walls, mismatched furniture with all sorts of stuff piled up on it, a beat-up old wooden coffee table, hardly anything on the walls. And plenty of dust.

She had gotten a glance inside the kitchen too, where every inch of counter space not occupied by dirty dishes or take-out containers was covered in crumbs large enough to see from across the room.

There was even a stale odor in the hall that led to the bedroom, like laundry that was well past needing to be washed. Thankfully that was faint, though, and easy enough to ignore.

She appreciated that the place didn't look anything like hers and Ron's. If it had, she'd probably be freaking out even more. She was clearheaded enough to realize that, at least.

Her head was throbbing again. It probably hadn't stopped, but she had forgotten about her sinus pain during the past hour's insanity. No matter. The headache hadn't forgotten.

"Yeah," she said, her face blank, her eyes not entirely focused. "Umm, can you do me a favor and please don't open the door? The front door, I mean. Except for the cops."

"Don't worry," Carter said. "Hey, maybe you want to take a shower? There are towels in that closet there, and I can get you something clean to wear."

"That's what I was just thinking. Thanks."

He seemed to believe her. That was something. She wasn't sure she believed what had just happened herself.

In retrospect, short time ago that it was, she should have realized something was wrong with Ron. She should've known something was up before he even got home. But she had been wrapped up in trying to fall asleep, and then, when that didn't work out, trying to get some action. Her hormones had bitten her in the ass again. She should have stopped everything when he refused to say a word. Maybe the end result wouldn't have been any different, but she probably wouldn't feel quite so dumb about things now.

When she'd felt the moisture on Ron's shirt, how wet and sticky his chest was, a million thoughts had raced through her head. Had he spilled a drink? Puked on himself? Fallen into a trash heap on the way home? But she never would have been able to conceive of the reality.

She had circled around the foot of the bed, angry he wasn't talking, frustrated her orgasm had taken a left turn out of town, and anxious to see what the story was with her boyfriend.

And then she had flipped the light on. And there he was, lying on the bed, reaching out with both arms, grasping at the air, reaching out for her, wearing nothing but a blood-soaked half-buttoned shirt and a hard-on.

And all of this *without a head.*

Linzy had gasped rather than screamed in that moment, unsure deep down if what she was seeing was real. How could it be? How could her boyfriend, whom she loved dearly, be lying in their bed, flailing about without a head?

There was no depression in the center of the pillow. It was almost as if the pillow had been covering his face up. But no, his neck was where he ended, the skin shredded in uneven tatters, as if something even more violent than your run-of-the-mill decapitation had occurred. But what? That's what had, and still, made no sense to Linzy. *What had happened? And when? And how was he seemingly alive without a head?* She knew the saying about chickens running around, but how long could such a thing last? This had to be something else.

And how was it this neighbor of hers—what was his name, *Carson?*—had believed her?

Or had he? Maybe he was just being kind, trying not to upset the clearly hysterical woman from the other end of the hall any further. Even if he didn't believe what she had told him, it had to be obvious she had been through some kind of traumatic event. And so he did what any good person would, and he took her in to relative safety. He was attempting to call the police. He was offering her hospitality. She would remember all of this.

Of course she would. It would be tough to forget anything about this night.

Linzy showered and changed into a t-shirt and some shorts her neighbor had fetched for her, saying the shorts had been left behind by an ex-girlfriend. They didn't fit quite right, of course—both garments were too big for her tiny frame—but she was happy to be in clean clothes.

He offered his bedroom to her, thinking she might want to sleep, and she accepted. It took a little while, but eventually she passed out.

Carter remained awake through the early morning hours, shaken enough by the events of the last hour or so, on top of his usual insomnia—though his experience encountering this woman Linzy in the hallway was nothing compared to what she had described seeing. He wondered if she was on something. It didn't seem like it. She seemed genuine, wild as her story was.

Finally, after what seemed like another hour, he got through to a 911 operator who told him they would dispatch the police as soon as they were able. It had been a particularly violent night all over the city, so she hadn't been able to give any sort of ETA. But it didn't matter.

HEADLESS

He was awake for the foreseeable future.

He pulled his laptop closer and hit play on the new Aphex Twin tracks he had downloaded and added to the top of his current playlist. He leaned his head back on the couch cushion as the beeps and boops and squelches drowned out the distant sirens and the whirring of the air conditioner and became the soundtrack to the last hours before sunrise.

FOUR

Tyree Pendleton: In Marleyville last night, a local resident contacted police, claiming to have seen a man get decapitated near the North End train station. But upon arrival on the scene, police said there was no body found, and instead the resident was arrested and charged with filing a false police report.

It was just one of a number of strange instances to occur all over the city last night. In a moment we'll go to Fiona Driscoll for more on this, but first, let's take a look at weather and traffic. Kat, how's the forecast looking?

Kat Vasquez: Well, Ty, we've certainly seen better days. It's hot, it's muggy, and we're going to see more rain before the end of rush hour. Take a look at this storm system moving across the country right now . . .

FIVE

JOANNA WAS UP EARLY. THIS was typical on Wednesdays, her mid-week day off, even though she rarely got out of the house as quickly as she liked.

Her Wednesday morning routine generally consisted of a slightly-earlier-than-usual trip to the gym, followed by a stop at Ground War, the anarchist coffee shop down the street where she liked to get a cheese danish and an iced cafe mocha, which negated most of the hard work she had put in at the gym. Probably all of it. *Definitely* all of it, and then some.

From there she would drive across the state line, about thirty minutes to Bailey's Notch. And every week she hoped her car, an ancient Toyota Camry, would hold out. One of these days, she was going to need to get some work done on it, or the thing was going to die on her, but she'd been putting it off. She didn't have tons of extra money, but what she did have, she was happier spending on iced coffee and sweets.

Technically she lived within the city limits, but she was right on the perimeter, in the Oak Park neighborhood, an area that felt both urban and suburban in certain ways. There were great restaurants, kitschy shops, art galleries, bars, nightlife, and everything else you could want from a city, but there were also things like easy access to parking and grocery stores, neither of which she'd ever had when she lived downtown. Plus it was relatively quiet, despite the number of people who lived there. Her current neighborhood was a nice middle ground. "Like a small town with a big city name," she would tell people who weren't familiar with the area.

But she liked taking her weekly drive to Bailey's Notch. It was good for clearing her head, and some of the scenery was beautiful. Gas was a lot cheaper out there too.

On the way there, she passed the building that used to house Newgan Media, the first "real" place she had worked after moving east, on the heels of getting kicked out of her parents' house by her less-than-understanding father. Back when she had a different name.

Newgan was a film distribution company that specialized in reissuing old, forgotten television shows on DVD. The company name, Newgan, was the surname of the founder, who had also turned it into a play on words, as evidenced by their slogan, "*Everything Old is Newgan*".

They got by for years because most of what they released was in the public domain, meaning licensing fees were nonexistent. But for reasons no one in the company could fathom, the owner had been staunchly resistant to upgrading their catalog from DVD to Blu-ray, not to mention firmly against the very idea of streaming video. And so, eventually, after years of declining profits, the company went bust.

Joanna had left the company for greener pastures before any of that took place, but for a while, she would occasionally hear from some of her old coworkers, and they'd get together over drinks to complain about how the place was run. Once Newgan closed up shop, though, she never heard from those people again, almost as if they had been discontinued along with the company's catalog of releases.

A few minutes outside the city, it was practically another world. Lots of farmland, interspersed with suburban housing developments. As she rolled into Bailey's Notch, it was all cornfields and cow fields, with occasional wooded stretches. From time to time, she would spot an entrance to a housing development in the middle of those woods. Elaborate signs would advertise Willow Glen, Brookside Commons, or Pine Hill. All the names were so generic and bland, and she wasn't even sure they corresponded to the sort of land they were on. She was happy she didn't live out here, but it was nice enough to visit.

A little further down the road, it was farmland again. She passed a large swath of fenced-in fields populated by cows. Somewhere along the way, she spotted some sort of animal—she couldn't tell what—lying dead in a patch of unkempt grass on the side of the road. If she had to guess, she'd say it was a dog, but it could have just as easily been something else. A small deer, perhaps, or maybe even a fox. But she didn't get a good enough look speeding by, with the creature's body obscured by the grass. She did notice, however, its midsection had a large chunk missing from it. She cringed at the sight and, distracted, didn't even notice the ambulance and its flashing lights approaching on the other side of the road. The siren squawked just before the two vehicles crossed paths, jarring Joanna and causing her to tense and squeeze the steering wheel tighter for a second. Then the moment passed and the ambulance was speeding off in her rearview mirror.

A few minutes later, she finally arrived at her destination, Mickey Dee's Farm Stand. She had been coming here for a few months. It was the best so-called hidden secret in the greater metropolitan area—though it was really only "hidden" in the sense that most folks from the city either didn't know about it or didn't bother with anything suburban, let alone something in farmland, even if it wasn't that far outside the city. But for people local to this area, Mickey Dee's was practically a regional treasure. Produce heaven. Some people further upstate would travel an hour or more just to pick up a bushel of apples or some of their famed tomatoes. And their sweet corn was unreal.

Joanna loved sweets—as a child, she had always claimed dessert as her favorite meal of the day—but she was trying to do better, and she had come to really enjoy certain fruits and vegetables. Plus, it was good to get out of the city every now and then, if only to breathe in some less-polluted air.

Mickey and his wife, Gwyneth, were third generation farmers, not to mention pillars of the community, having expanded their family's operation significantly over the years. The so-called Farm Stand had literally started as a table on the side of the main road decades earlier, before expanding to two tables, then four tables and a refrigerated case, and so on. Now, it was a massive open-air market with a roof to shield everything from rain and a parking lot that could accommodate dozens of vehicles. When the lot filled up, as it often did, people just parked along the street beyond it.

It was busy every time Joanna stopped by, but she had found early Wednesday mornings were a bit less so, for some reason she never managed to figure out, so she had made the journey part of her weekly routine. She had Wednesdays off anyway, so it worked out perfectly.

It wasn't just the produce. She had come to develop a nice rapport with Gwyneth, Mickey's wife, and she enjoyed chatting with her for a few minutes each week about what was happening in each other's lives.

The place was surprisingly empty this morning. Normally there were at least ten or fifteen people milling about, even this early in the day in the middle of the week. But today, Joanna only spotted three other people among the produce as she roamed the aisles, and one of them was Mickey himself.

Joanna didn't particularly like Mickey. He was fine, she supposed, but he generally gave off a grumpy vibe. Maybe that was just the way he was. Or maybe it was her. Wouldn't be the first time her mere existence had put someone—particularly an older, conservative white man—on their heels. She had experienced that a lot ever since she'd been out on her own.

Gwyneth was nowhere to be found today, however, and for that, Joanna was sorry. She enjoyed their conversations, even when they were brief and without much substance. But sometimes it was good to simply have a nice chat with nice people. Joanna didn't have a huge social network since Newgan Media had shut down, so any chance at pleasant human interaction was welcome. She had her own little community in the city, sure, but it was nice to get along with people who were very much cut from a different cloth too.

Joanna felt the pressure of her shopping basket's handles in the crook of her elbow as she loaded it up. She'd have to stop soon. She was single and lived alone, and there was only so much she could eat in a week. Plus she knew half of whatever she bought was going to go to rot anyway. She liked the idea of eating vegetables more than the actual act of it.

"Hiya, Joe," Mickey said as she approached the checkout. As usual, he rubbed her the wrong way right off the bat.

"It's *Joanna,*" she responded. She probably should've expected this. She wasn't happy to see Mickey's eyes roll when she contradicted him. It was as if he was saying "whatever," and that pissed her off.

Still, it wasn't as if Mickey was a total grump. He had to interact with customers all the time and couldn't afford to be too much of an asshole, she figured.

"No Gwyneth today?" Joanna tried to keep things light.

"Nah, she's in bed."

"Aww, sorry to hear that. Tell her I said hi, and I hope she gets better soon."

"Oh, she'll be fine," Mickey said, almost dismissively. "Just a headache. Rain's comin' back. She always gets this way before a storm." He looked through the roof, which was made of thick plexiglass rather than wood and shingles, to the west, from where the gray clouds were approaching.

"Well, I suppose I'll see her next week."

"You oughta try some of our purple sweet potatoes," Mickey said, as he bagged Joanna's selections.

"Oh?"

"Hearty vegetable. Put some hair on your chest, as we used to say." Mickey chuckled to himself. Another customer, a tall man who appeared to be in his mid-fifties, approached and set his mostly empty basket down while he waited. Mickey turned his way. "Is that all for you today, Hank? I was just telling Joe here about our purple sweet potatoes. Very robust. Fill ya with vitamins and vigor, if you know what I'm sayin'."

Hank smiled politely but didn't comment.

"Sure I can't interest you in some, Joe?"

"I'm good, thanks. And it's Joanna, Mickey. Please."

Mickey looked up for a second and met Joanna's glare. They locked eyes and she held it, along with her breath, until he looked back down and finished loading her haul into the tote bag she had supplied. Then Mickey motioned to the total on the register's display and she paid him from the wad of cash she had haphazardly stuffed into the back pocket of her cutoffs. She finally exhaled when she reached the parking lot, her feet crunching on the gravel.

She could hear Mickey muttering to Hank through the open air as she approached her car. At first she wasn't able to hear the individual words, but then, suddenly, something came through crystal clear.

"These fuckin' gender-benders or whatever ya call 'em," she heard him say. "No sense of humor at all."

The words brought her to a standstill. She wasn't looking for a fight today. She wasn't looking for one any day, really. But of every process one had to go through in life, buying food should be simple, straightforward, and completely devoid of any drama. We were all humans after all, and despite what our personal circumstances and lived experiences were, no matter how much money any of us made or how many people we had depending on us or any of that shit, we all had to eat. Buying food should not have any baggage attached to it, shouldn't be a source of pain or misery or ill feelings for anyone. And yet, here she was, bruised from some small-minded man's completely unnecessary comments.

She stood there a moment, debating what, if anything, to do. Was it worth it? Was this man going to change his mind in light of anything she had to say to him?

SIX

LINZY WOKE TO THE SOUND of a chainsaw. It took a second to register, but when it did, her eyes shot open. This was not a normal sound to hear in the city, morning or otherwise. Then she remembered she had woken to the same sound the day before. A crew was trimming some fallen tree limbs in and around the park down the street.

It also took her a second to recognize she was not in her own bed, nor was she wearing her own clothes. She had slept on top of the covers.

Reality settled in quickly, though, as she felt the itchiness on her arms, a result of using someone else's regular soap on her sensitive skin. She remembered the events of last night, though she still couldn't believe them.

In the distance, beyond the chainsaw, she heard someone yelling and wondered if they were complaining about the work crew's noise. In the city, there was always someone, somewhere, grumbling about or criticizing every little thing. Not that there weren't nice people too. In fact, the nicer ones far outnumbered the crazies in her experience. But you never heard about them in the news.

A siren also sounded outside, and she wondered if her neighbor, Carter, whose bed she had slept in, had ever gotten through to 911. She wondered if he was even awake.

The cushy carpet of his bedroom floor felt good beneath her bare feet, a small dose of comfort in an otherwise nightmarish past few hours.

She padded across the room, noticing the piles of clothes heaped all along the edges of the space, and the disorganized state of the dresser, and the lack of a mirror, then unlocked the bedroom door and cracked it open slowly. Carter was on the couch, watching the morning news on TV.

"Hey, good morning," he said, sitting up from his slouched position, his voice pleasant but obviously filled with concern for her. That was sweet. "Did you sleep any?"

"Some. Not the greatest dreams." Her eyes settled back down to only half-open. Her voice, now that she heard it for the first time, was froggy.

"I just made coffee, if you want some. And I've got cereal. No eggs or anything special, but—oh, I could make oatmeal. I have some microwave packets somewhere."

"Coffee. Yes. Please." She prayed for it to be delivered in a clean mug.

"It took a while, but I finally talked to the police," Carter said on his way to the kitchen. "Well, a 911 dispatcher, technically. Apparently it was a crazy night, but they said since you're safe they'd send someone over ASAP, which I'm hoping means this morning. Cream?"

"Black, please. No sugar." Linzy planted herself on the couch and took a deep breath, processing the information. "Thank you," she said. "For everything."

"Hey, what are strangers for?" They both chuckled.

Carter returned to the couch and handed Linzy a mug. Steam floated off the top. She held it between her palms for a moment, feeling the contrast of the heat in her hands to the coolness of the apartment. It was much nicer than her place in that respect. How did this guy keep it so cool in here?

On TV, the news anchor was doing the seven-day forecast. Oppressive heat and periodic storms were a common theme. Linzy suddenly noticed her headache was back with a vengeance, pain encircling her eyes like a pair of too-tight goggles.

"Can I use your phone?" she asked. "I need to call my job and tell them I won't be in today."

"Sure, of course. Anything to eat?"

"Maybe some toast? And Advil if you have it."

Just as Carter was about to give his phone to Linzy, it buzzed in his hand. He answered the call, holding a finger up to her as he made his way back to the kitchen. The conversation was quick, and he hung up as he pulled two slices of bread out and dropped them into the toaster.

"Cops are here, actually," he said. "Umm, I'm gonna go down and meet them in the lobby. Butter's right here, and there's strawberry preserves in the fridge if you want 'em. Advil's in the medicine cabinet. Cool?"

Linzy nodded.

"Great. I'll be right back."

By the time Carter returned, Linzy was finishing the last bite of her toast. She took a moment to swallow a couple Advil before greeting the officers who accompanied him.

"Good morning, Miss . . . ?" the taller of the two cops began.

"Oh, it's Dunlop. Linzy Dunlop."

"Good morning, Miss Dunlop. I'm Officer Treadwell, and this is my partner, Officer Kilmeade. We understand there was an incident in your apartment last night." The cops looked tired and vaguely annoyed, but maybe that was just their default.

Linzy took a deep breath and told them the story. She told them about Ron being out late. About how it was too hot to sleep. About how he'd stumbled home, seemingly drunk. She told them she had initiated sex and how Ron had complied but hadn't said a word. She had never been shy discussing her sex life but didn't see the need to go into too much detail. Then she told them about feeling the wetness on Ron's shirt and turning on the light. And how that was the moment she realized Ron's head had been chopped off. How he was still flailing around—kicking, if not screaming—like he wasn't actually dead yet. How he had swiped at her. How he had actually grabbed her arm and pulled with great strength. And she talked about being able to get away, and how she had eventually found a kind soul in Carter.

As she explained the events of the early morning hours, she expected the officers to be dismissive and condescending, but all things considered, they weren't. They asked questions—including whether or not she had taken any drugs the night before—but she was surprised how professional they acted toward her.

"Well, why don't we go take a look?" Officer Treadwell said. And they did. Linzy wasn't exactly thrilled to return to the apartment. She was terrified about what the scene looked like and didn't want to see the body of her dead boyfriend again, but she took a few more deep breaths and girded herself for the moment. It helped to have other people accompany her. But her knees felt wobbly anyway.

As they walked down the hall, the officers noted several marks on the walls and spots on the floor, all of which had the distinct reddish-brown color of dried blood. Linzy hadn't remembered touching so many surfaces on her frantic journey, but she supposed it was possible. She also didn't realize quite how far she had gone before someone had opened their door to her. She was always surprised at the size of the building in which she resided. She only ever thought of the confines of her and Ron's own tiny part of it.

They walked down the long hall, passing the elevators and fire stairs, then turned left at the corner, passed by the garbage room, and continued almost all the way to the end, where Linzy's apartment sat. Number 216, on the right.

She hadn't remembered closing the door on her way out. She only remembered running.

Linzy turned the knob—the door was unlocked—but it was Officers Treadwell and Kilmeade who entered first.

"It's to the left," she said, indicating the direction of the bedroom, as if they wouldn't be able to figure it out themselves. It wasn't that big of a place. She entered the apartment too, trailing slowly behind them. Carter was right behind her. If her legs gave out, she wondered if he would catch her.

"Please don't touch anything," one of the cops said. Linzy wasn't sure which one.

There was blood on the inside of the door and the door frame, and several smeared footprints dried on the kitchen tile. More than she would've expected to see. She and Carter did their best to avoid stepping on any of it.

The officers spent plenty of time in the bedroom, but also looked in every other corner of the apartment—the kitchen, the living room, the bathroom, even the coat closet. Then one of them asked if she could come into the bedroom.

Crossing the threshold, she was able to see the state of things. The air conditioner was still humming. The upper portion of the bed was covered with blood, most of which had dried, staining the gray sheets a deep crimson, which looked black in the wrinkles and folds. There were spatters and smears on the headboard. And the pillowcase was an entirely new color.

But there was no body. Ron was gone.

That's when Linzy's legs finally did give out. She didn't fall—she simply collapsed into a squat before tipping back onto her butt. She sat back, leaned against the closet doors, and brought a hand to her mouth.

What the fuck? What the fuck was going on? What was this?

Her boyfriend, whom she had sent off to work with a kiss twenty-four hours earlier, had somehow returned home last night, gotten himself decapitated at some point, had sex with her, *and somehow attacked her in the process?* And now his had-to-be-dead body was . . . *missing? What the fuck?*

The officers asked Linzy a number of questions, and she answered them, but seconds later, she had forgotten every word. More sirens passed outside and a call had come in over the officers' radio. She only heard the words "all units," and a moment later, they were gone.

"How many fucking things like this are we gonna see today?" Officer Kilmeade said to his partner as they descended the fire stairs to the ground floor. "It's not even nine a.m. for fuck's sake!"

Carter helped Linzy stand up. He relayed what the officers had said before leaving—how they ought to leave the apartment as is and go elsewhere for the time being. That they'd be in touch later for further questioning, and that another crew would probably show up at some point soon to take more comprehensive photos. They had said not to leave town.

Linzy rubbed her eyes and tried to clear the cobwebs of her half-catatonic state. Utter disbelief. And no answers.

Back on her feet, she opened the closet, where she quickly assembled some clothes and put them in a tote bag. Then she grabbed her phone off the dresser, where it was still plugged in, and some underwear from a drawer.

She closed the door for a minute so she could change into some of her own clothes. In the process, she accidentally touched the smear of dried blood on the inside, and a chill ran down her spine, replaying the events that had led to where they were now.

She got changed as quickly as she could, trying to avoid looking beyond her own image in the mirror. She didn't want to see the bed again, or the stains on the sheets.

"I'll wash these and get them back to you soon," she said through the door to Carter, wanting to make some sort of conversation so she didn't feel quite so alone in the room.

She was going to have to move. There was no way she'd be able to sleep in this room ever again.

"Don't worry about it," he said. "The shirt doesn't fit me anymore, and the shorts belonged to an ex. You can keep 'em or toss 'em. Use 'em for rags if you want."

Soon, she was dressed and ready to leave. She grabbed her bag and asked Carter if it was okay to stash it at his place.

On the way out, she got her keys from the dish on the living room table and locked the apartment up like it was a tomb being preserved for museum study.

Perhaps it was all the blood, but neither Linzy, nor Carter, nor the cops had noticed the little translucent rubbery things on the mattress, beneath the edge of the pillow, or on the floor, just below the side rail of the bed frame. There weren't many of them. Just a few. They looked like grains of rice, with tiny ridges, but made of something like silicone.

And they *squirmed.*

SEVEN

JOANNA SAT IN THE DRIVER'S seat of her Camry, fuming. The door was open and she had one leg out, uncommitted to either driving away or getting back out. The frayed edge of her cutoff jean shorts fluttered in the soft breeze, tickling her thigh. She was pissed off. She wanted to march right back to the Mickey Dee's cash register, get in that old farmer's face and give him a piece of her mind.

This wasn't the first time she had been looked at funny or spoken to derisively. She was used to that. But the way he had glared at her, treated her dismissively, and even called her by that name. "*Joe.*" Not to mention what he had said as she walked away.

Part of her wanted to rearrange the guy's face. But more than that, she wished there was a way to force people to have some compassion.

A man and woman, both extremely tall and slender, walked lazily through the gravel parking lot, wide smiles on their faces as their sandals crunched the stones beneath their feet. They had matching light-brown hair that hung straight, reaching the middles of their backs, and they wore tie-dyed shirts and what appeared to be vintage bell-bottoms, like a pair of hippies straight out of the late 1960s or early '70s. The woman puffed on a joint and passed it to the man, then they both exploded with laughter, pausing to double over for a second before continuing to float toward the farm stand.

Joanna took note of them but didn't hear what was said. They weren't talking about her, she could tell that much. They seemed to be in their own little world.

She was happy for it. That's all she wanted in life. To be left alone. To not be regarded as a menace or considered a freak. To simply exist in peace.

Why couldn't people just live and let live? Why did everyone have to be so concerned with everyone else's every move, every breath, what they did in their bedrooms, and how they chose to dress?

The hippies had that love-one-another shit right, if nothing else.

Gwyneth had never shown Joanna anything but respect. She was kind and loving. And she was of the same generation as Mickey, so it wasn't entirely accurate to say he was simply a man from another time. People were capable of change. Perhaps with a nudge in the right direction, they could become more compassionate. They just needed to see the human, and the heart, inside each of us.

That was it, she decided. She would go back to the register. But she wasn't going to yell at Mickey. She was going to talk to him, peacefully. As best as she could.

But as she walked across the parking lot, she thought to herself, why is the burden on me? Why should I have to do the work to make him a better person? She was getting riled up again. She was livid before she even got to the checkout area.

The hippies were standing off to the side.

"Like, it's a potato?" one of them said. "But it's . . . *sweet*?" Then they both burst into laughter again.

"*Hey, Mickey!*" Joanna shouted. She paid no attention to the customer he was helping at the time. This couldn't wait.

The farmer glanced in Joanna's direction and held up a finger to indicate he needed a moment to finish what he was doing.

"No, Mickey, this is important," she said as she continued her approach.

"Take it easy, Joe. I'll be with you in just a minute."

There it was again. *That name.*

"Goddammit, Mickey, I told you my name is Joanna!" Blood rushed to her head instantly; her face grew red in a flash. She was so mad, she felt like she was going to burst.

"Now you listen here, *Joe-Anna!* I'm trying to run a business here, and I don't need you to come at me screaming like a banshee when I'm in the middle of helping a customer! These are good hardworking people, and . . ."

Joanna tuned out then. She knew it was going to be a screaming match, knew it was going to be contentious. It already had been. But something about the moment struck her as off. Mickey's words turned to abrasive noise in her ears as she watched his face expand and contract and contort with his angry retort. She watched the double chin he tried to hide beneath his scruffy white beard jiggle too. But it wasn't any of that that threw her. It was the color his face turned—it went red, then purple, then beyond in mere seconds. And it was the way the upper half of his head seemed to quickly be swelling.

A second or two later, it happened. Mickey was in the middle of a sentence when his words, or at least his voice, suddenly failed him. His eyes grew wide and stretched into some ungodly shape as his cheeks puffed out and his ears tilted in a way Joanna had never seen happen before.

And just like that, the farmer's head exploded, like a water balloon dropped from twelve stories up. Blood, bone, and brain matter splattered across the register and the stand on which it sat, splashing the customer he had been helping, and painting the crates of sweet corn behind him. Red goo drenched the front of Mickey's overalls as gobs of brain and flesh and tufts of hair rained down all around.

"Ah man, my tie-dye!" shouted one of the hippies.

But that wasn't the craziest thing that happened in the moment. The craziest thing was the way Mickey Dee's headless body attempted to crawl over the counter and head toward Joanna, like he was still furious with her for interrupting his business.

It took a moment, but Mickey's body finally did clear the counter, though it moved awkwardly, knocking his customer's selection of vegetables to the floor in the process. The confused patron took a step back from the action and tripped over his own feet, falling back onto a display of butternut squash.

Mickey's body stumbled then too, nearly collapsing to the ground before standing upright again and pausing. Joanna froze for a second, trying to process what was happening, as Mickey's body flexed its arms a couple times, as if to make sure they were still working properly. Then the body began moving toward her, taking herky-jerky steps, seemingly unsure of its ability to move in a balanced way.

Joanna found the will to unstick her feet and ran. As she dashed toward the parking lot, then through it to her car, she realized the sky had gone fully gray. Thunder sounded in the distance, and the first few drops of rain began to fall as she slammed the car door closed.

She looked back and saw Mickey's headless body still coming for her as she popped the key into the ignition and hoped the car would start.

EIGHT

I AM BORN.
We are born.
And we will do all we can to grow. To expand. To take over.
We enter. We pass through tissue. We ride bloodstreams.
We find the brain.
And we swell. We emit. We plant our seeds.
I am born.
I will birth.

NINE

Operator: 911, what's your emergency?

Caller: Hey, uh, like, there's this guy, and his head, like, *exploded*?

Operator: What's your location? Can you give me an address?

Caller: We're at the farm stand on Route . . . something . . .

Operator: Are you currently somewhere safe?

Caller: I guess. Like, we're just hanging out behind the eggplants. Is that what these are called? *Eggplants?* That doesn't sound right. Eggplants.

Person in background: Some people say 'aubergines.'

Caller: Auger *what*? Egger? *Egger*-jeans?

Operator: Are there other people with you?

Caller: Just my lady. And some other people.

Operator: Is there a shooter?

Caller: Nah, I don't think so. Just, like, some other people who wanted to get some vegetables.

Operator: What's happening right now?

Caller: So this guy, Mike I think his name is . . . He's, like, a farmer, and he was just, like, getting all mad at some lady, and his face got all red and his head just, like, went [blows raspberries]. And now he just took off down the road. But like, with *no head*! He's literally running around like a chicken with his head cut off!

Operator: Sir . . .

Caller: *Whoa . . . wait . . .* maybe it was the chickens getting, like, revenge or something?

Person in background: *Whoooaaa.*

Operator: Sir, have you taken any drugs in the past twenty-four hours?

Caller: Miss, it's starting to rain. I gotta go. [more faintly] Eggplants? *Really?* But they're *purple . . .*

[call ends]

TEN

MICKEY'S BODY WASN'T MOVING TERRIBLY fast. Without a head, that wasn't surprising. But still, how many steps should a headless human body be able to take anyway?

Joanna didn't spend much time thinking about it. She jumped in her car as quickly as she could and got the fuck out of dodge. She turned the ignition—thankfully the car started right away—and peeled out, kicking up gravel as her tires found the traction to leave. She flipped on the headlights and wipers as soon as she exited the parking lot and turned onto the main road.

She could see Mickey's body in her rearview, made blurry by the raindrops that had begun to fall, still moving unsteadily in her direction. How had he not simply collapsed yet?

What a morning it had been already. This was not the way she expected her day off to go. All the anger she had felt just a few minutes ago had suddenly been replaced by this other feeling, this flee-the-scene sort of panic. She didn't feel safe out here in the 'burbs any longer.

She drove, and drove fast. All she wanted to do at this point was get home. She stepped on the gas even harder, moving as quickly as she could without losing control of the car. She passed the fields of cows and corn, and the entrances to all the housing developments hidden back in the woods. She'd be back to the city, back in her apartment soon enough. As long as her car held out.

Twenty minutes passed and so far, so good.

The rain began to pick up a bit as she crossed the state line and got back into the city limits. The more it did, though, the more her wipers struggled to clear it. The rain seemed slimy somehow, her windshield almost looked like it was covered with a thin film of Vaseline, her view smeared. Or was it a problem with the wipers themselves? Shit, one more thing to fix. This thing was a heap. She wished she could afford a new car.

She turned the wiper control to increase the speed as she prepared to turn onto Oak Park Avenue. Up ahead, at the intersection, about to walk into traffic, was a man in a three-piece suit, just like her father used to wear. His shoulders were broad, and the top of his suit was stained a brilliant crimson. Even through the blurry glass, it was easy enough to see: *He had no head.*

No. She had to be seeing things. Or imagining things. Right? It was the rain, and her suddenly defective wipers, and the stress of what she had experienced. It had to be.

She couldn't wait to get home and crawl under a blanket, maybe call her therapist. Just a few more blocks and she'd be there.

But when she reached the intersection, the guy without a head stepped right into her path.

ELEVEN

CARTER HAD SUGGESTED GETTING A proper breakfast at a diner he knew across town, and Linzy agreed, since the toast she had eaten at his apartment had not been nearly enough. She had never even heard of the place he brought her to, but it turned out to be incredible. Her belly full, it turned out to be exactly what she needed, at least for the moment. She slumped down in her seat, tiny on her side of the maroon, faux-leather booth.

The place was packed. Silverware clatter and conversation filled the air, along with the aromas of eggs, fried potatoes, and salty breakfast meats.

Carter had ordered the French toast, complimented by a bowl of grits and a side of scrapple. Linzy had gone with the Big Break #3, which consisted of two eggs (sunny side up), home fries (well done), a short stack of pancakes (silver dollar style), and sausage (vegetarian).

While they waited for the check to arrive, Linzy suddenly realized she had never alerted anyone at work that she wouldn't be in today. She had seen a hundred notifications on her phone when she'd grabbed it out of her apartment, but so far hadn't bothered to look at most of them. They were probably mostly social media alerts or

DoorDash coupon codes anyway, maybe a text or two from some scammer telling her about a fake charge to her Amazon account or offering a free vacation if she would only confirm a few details.

All she had looked for, even knowing it wouldn't be there, was a text from Ron. She desperately hoped she had been hallucinating last night, or that the events of the early morning hours were part of some elaborate dream she still hadn't woken from. But no.

She texted Ron anyway. *Babe r u ok?* She knew she wouldn't receive a response, but she wanted to send the message despite the reality. Sometimes people prayed for the impossible, knowing full well it was impossible, hoping for a one-in-a-million chance at a miracle, or at least some confluence of fortuitous accidental circumstances.

She had a series of texts from Sheinelle, one of her coworkers. She dashed off a response, asking her to tell their boss she needed to take a personal day, and that she'd give more details later. Then she followed that up with a second text, saying she'd probably need to take the rest of the week off, and that her boyfriend was missing.

Missing his head.

A knot in Linzy's stomach twisted.

"You wanna go walk around some more when we're done here?" Carter offered, sipping his third cup of coffee. Maybe that was why he had trouble sleeping at night. "There's a lot of great shops and stuff on this street and the next one over. I've got some work I need to get done at some point, but my schedule's flexible."

Linzy had set her phone on the table, face-down, and was staring out the window of the diner.

"It's raining," she said. She took a gulp from her own coffee mug and realized her headache had finally dissipated a bit. Maybe it was the Advil she had taken, or maybe it was the food, or the caffeine. Or maybe it was that the rain had finally started. That was usually the way it went. Pressure built up beforehand, and then the rain was like a release.

Their waitress returned. "Anything else I can get for you today? Another refill?"

"I think we're good," Carter responded. He looked to Linzy, who was still staring outside, but she didn't say anything.

"Okay then. I'll just leave the check here. No rush."

The windows had begun to fog. Even so, Linzy felt like she could see through the glass clearly enough. There were people running about, many without umbrellas, attempting to travel to their destinations without getting too soaked. But she was focused on the man standing across the street, at the corner of the intersection. He was wearing a suit, which looked out of place in this slightly more bohemian section of the city. He seemed hesitant, lifting one leg as if he was about to step off the sidewalk before setting it back down again, and then repeating the process. He seemed to have his head down too, or at least that's how it looked from behind. His broad shoulders were darker than the rest of his suit, no doubt bearing the brunt of the rain. If he didn't move soon, he was likely to get drenched all the way through.

"I guess we can sit here a few more minutes and see if it passes," Carter said as he scanned over the bill. "I didn't even think to bring an umbrella."

The man on the corner turned and jumped into the middle of the intersection. His movements were uneven, unsteady, but he seemed to move quickly. And Linzy could see now that the man had no head.

Just like Ron.

Her eyes went wide and a short gasp escaped her throat as she pressed hard into the cushion of her seat with both palms. She continued to stare. Even through the foggy glass and from a distance, she could see the raggedness of the man's neck, in particular one large flap of blood-soaked skin draped over his collar, his ear still connected to it, lying limp on his shoulder.

"What do you think?" Carter asked. He looked up and saw the look in her eyes. "Hey, you okay?" Then he looked where she was looking and saw the last moment of the man entering the intersection. And the dingy old Camry that careened around the corner.

The vehicle skidded, quickly losing traction on the wet pavement as it tried to make the turn and avoid the pedestrian. But it was no use. The car was no match for the slippery road, and momentum tipped it onto its passenger side, sending it sliding into the headless man, then into the front of another car, pushing all of them toward the curb on the other side of the street.

TWELVE

"HEY! GET BACK HERE! YOU didn't pay your bill!" The waitress ran out the front door of the diner, chasing after her patrons. She wasn't excited about getting soaked, but the owner had been coming down hard on all the employees lately, instituting a new policy that docked the waitstaff for anything lost to dine-and-dashers. She wasn't even sure that was legal, but she felt she had to chase anyone she thought she had a chance at catching. And she had spotted these two running out the door right away. One of the busboys had joined her.

Linzy and Carter hadn't intended to skip out on their check, but when the car accident happened, Linzy jumped into action and Carter had followed right after.

As he jogged behind Linzy, Carter pulled his phone out to call 911 again, hoping he'd be able to get through right away this time.

Traffic had stopped, but there was a cacophony of horns blaring among the sounds of the rain hitting the ground. Still, through all the noise, Carter heard the waitress' voice. From the middle of the road, he turned back just in time to see her point him out to the busboy, only for the kid to move in his direction and slip on the wet pavement, his feet flying out from underneath him. He landed hard on his left hip and winced. Even from a distance Carter could see the grimace on the guy's face. He stopped for a second in the middle of the street and debated running back to help him, but the waitress and a few others on the sidewalk came to his aid immediately.

The phone kept trilling in his ear. No one was picking up. Had he dialed correctly? He glanced at his screen to be sure, but of course he had. It was only three digits. Then he looked back toward the diner and saw people backing away from the busboy, who was now on his knees. Carter's jaw dropped as he watched what happened next.

The kid's body seemed to shiver—maybe just an effect of the cool rain—but that was nothing compared to his face. Even from Carter's vantage point dozens of feet away, he could see the way the boy's cheeks were moving—expanding and rippling, undulating like ocean waves. His forehead seemed to be swelling too, turning purple. Had he hit his head on the pavement?

He closed his eyes briefly, but they opened wide a second later, perhaps against his will. One of them grew large enough that it had no choice but to escape its socket, slumping lazily over the edge of his lower eyelid and onto his swollen cheek as a trail of red drooled out from behind it. He opened his mouth to scream, but the sound of his voice was cut off by the spontaneous explosion half a second later. Even from where he stood, through everything else that was happening, Carter could hear the wet splat of the poor guy's brain and skull as countless tiny pieces hit the sidewalk all at once, decorating it with an abstract design that began to run in the rain.

Carter stood there in shock, phone still to his ear. He hadn't entirely believed every word of Linzy's story until that moment. It was obvious something awful had happened, but what exactly had remained a mystery in his mind. He knew she wasn't a murderer. But it wasn't until this moment that he had believed everything she had said about her boyfriend's missing head.

He gave up on 911 and tucked the phone into the narrow pocket of his shorts made specifically for it and ran to the site of the crashed cars, where Linzy was helping a woman out of the Camry on its side.

A small group of people were attending to the other car, but most of them had their hands over their mouths. It didn't look like a good scene, and he was sure there was nothing he could do to help there.

So he ran to the car where Linzy was. He arrived just as the driver, with Linzy's help, had climbed fully out through the shattered side window. She was wearing a tank top and a pair of cutoff jean shorts, and she was grasping a mini backpack and a small canvas tote in one hand. Standing side by side, she was easily a head taller than Linzy, with long curls of dirty blonde hair, a few strands of which were stained red. She had a small dribble of blood on her forehead, which, in light of what he had just seen across the street, caused Carter's heart to stutter. But a breath later, he realized she had probably just bumped her head in the accident.

"Are you okay?" he asked, new on the scene.

"I think I'm fine," Joanna said. "A little banged up, but . . . I think I'm okay." Linzy had a hand on the woman's elbow and another wrapped behind her back, ready to catch her if she stumbled. What a morning this had been.

"Do you want to sit?" Linzy asked. There was a small park at the other end of the block. If the woman didn't want to sit on the curb, it wasn't too far to a bench, though maybe it would make more sense to go into the diner, out of the rain. "We can definitely get you to a hospital too."

The rain, which had never become terribly heavy, seemed to be easing up even further. Sirens wailed in the distance. A dog barked somewhere nearby too.

Joanna shook her head. "I'm good. But you wouldn't happen to have a tissue or a napkin or something, would you?"

Carter suddenly realized he'd been holding onto the check from the diner in his left hand. He gave it to the woman, who promptly used it to dab the cut on her hairline.

"Those sirens are getting louder. Someone will be here soon," Linzy said. Carter mentioned that he tried to call 911, but couldn't get through. Obviously someone else had.

He looked down at the pavement and noted the scattered chunks of glass and plastic in the road and on the sidewalk. Were some of them . . . *moving*? No, it was just the rain making everything seem that way.

Behind them, at the other crashed car, a man screamed. Most of his body was hidden behind the wreck, but Carter, Linzy, and Joanna all watched as he seemed to struggle with someone. An arm extended through the window of the inverted sedan and clutched the front of the man's shirt. The man outside swiped and swung at the person inside, throwing amateur looping punches while trying to pull away, until finally he escaped the person's grasp. He scrambled away from the scene as the others surrounding the car all gasped in horror at what they saw before scattering themselves.

Then Carter saw too. The driver of the vehicle crawled out. It was another man, in gray shorts and a red t-shirt. And he was headless.

"Oh fuck!" someone screamed. "Run!" yelled someone else.

The barking dog had gotten louder too, and suddenly it appeared from around the building on the corner. It was a fairly sizable Airedale, its fur brown and black. The dog leaned forward, its leash taut. It seemed to be dragging its person behind it. Finally a hand became visible from behind the corner, bound in a tangle of the leash, followed by an arm, then a body. *But no head.*

This one seemed to be a boy, a teenager maybe, in a horizontal-striped shirt covered with blood and gunk. Carter got a good look at the ragged flesh of the teen's neck, where his body ended. There were chunks of flesh and brain matter still stuck to his shirt, and as Carter stared, one of them became heavy enough to slide off and fall to the sidewalk with a splat. Carter fought to keep his scrapple down.

"Carter . . ."

The scene was incomprehensible. How could this be? *How were people walking around without their heads?* It made sense that a body might be able to move for a minute or two, but anything beyond that seemed well past the realm of possibility.

Carter glanced back in the direction of the diner. The busboy, headless, was moving right toward them. He wasn't fast, nor was he nimble, so they had that going for them at least.

"Carter . . ."

The Airedale continued tugging at the leash, trying with some success to lead the other headless boy where it wanted to go—which was also in their direction. The dog barked and barked, and then, in an instant . . . Splat. The barking stopped and everything above the dog's collar burst, sending chunks of bone and fur flying. The dog's body twisted side-to-side, as if to shake off some of the muck it had just painted its own body with, like one last conscious act, before stumbling over its own two front feet and collapsing to the ground.

"Carter! We need to go!" Linzy's voice finally broke through. "Now!"

She still had her arm around the other woman. Both of their faces wore urgent expressions.

"Yeah," Carter said softly, snapping back to life.

"My apartment's just a few blocks from here," Joanna said.

"I think we need to go somewhere else," Linzy responded.

"Things are looking pretty crazy around here. His car's over this way. You want to come with us?"

Joanna nodded, and the three of them ran.

THIRTEEN

"I'M JOANNA, BY THE WAY." She had been sitting in the back seat, behind the driver of the Honda Accord, for a few minutes, and nobody had said anything. She figured some introductions were in order, given the experience they'd all just had together.

"Nice to meet you, Joanna. Sorry. I'm Linzy." She turned around and offered a comforting smile.

"I'm Carter," the driver said, glancing through the rearview mirror as he navigated the wet streets back to where he and Linzy both lived.

"And this is one fucked up day, huh?" Linzy offered. She realized Joanna had no idea what they'd been through since the middle of the night. Of course, maybe Joanna had had a crazy night herself. They'd get into it eventually. But the statement stood, even if it had only referred to the car crash and the handful of headless people they had come up against at the scene.

It only took them ten minutes by car to get back to Linzy and Carter's neighborhood, but it might as well have been interplanetary travel. It was a completely different world. Things seemed much calmer here.

Along the way, they passed another car accident, with a public bus and a pickup truck both engulfed in flames. They also saw some people running down the street, who may have been fleeing some fearful situation, or just as easily may have been running late for appointments. And plenty of ambulances, fire trucks, and police vehicles had screamed past them with their sirens blaring. But the further they got from the area around the diner in Joanna's neighborhood, the calmer things seemed to be. Even the rain had stopped and the skies had partially cleared by the time they got across town.

Carter nevertheless circled the blocks surrounding the apartment building a few times, moving cautiously, as he and his two passengers surveyed the area, looking for anything that seemed dangerous or, at the very least, out of the ordinary.

Just to be safe, they decided not to park in the garage next to the building. If they had any reason to leave in a hurry, they wouldn't be able to get out of there fast enough, if at all. So Carter found a spot on the street about a block away.

"I just went shopping the other day, so my place is stocked with food," Carter said. They didn't say anything about it, but he and Linzy both knew they weren't going to her place, with the bloodsoaked sheets and the impending police investigation. But he was more than happy to host people for a couple days if that's what was needed. He might not keep the neatest house, but deep down he was a good guy. A good citizen. A good neighbor.

None of them knew what was going on, really, or how widespread any of it was. But it felt like the beginning of something big, or at least potentially big, like the early days of a pandemic. They'd been through that just a few years prior. Only this felt a little more chaotic and murderous.

Carter was the first to crack his door open. He did so slowly, the hinge creaking softly, and sat there for a moment, all three of them listening for trouble. When he opened it all the way, the other two followed suit.

It sounded like any other day. People were walking around, having conversations, going about their business. Cars and trucks were driving in all directions. The buzz of the city was there, just like any other day. There were sirens in the distance, but that was typical, a standard part of urban life many city dwellers didn't even notice when it wasn't pointed out to them.

Joanna had managed to fit the contents of her tote bag into her mini backpack, and she slipped the straps over her shoulders when she got out of the car. She didn't want to leave anything behind, in the event they got separated or she decided to go her own way. But for now, she was sticking with these people.

She noticed a bruise on her left arm, but other than that and the cut on her forehead, she didn't think she had suffered much from the accident. She'd pay attention to herself, though, in case something started to feel off. She'd felt more in tune with her body in recent years.

Thinking about it, she realized she did have a slight headache, but she was sure it wasn't a concussion. Probably just stress, with a little light jostling. She had banged her head on something, after all. But she knew it wasn't a concussion. She'd had a couple of those in her lifetime, and this, with the little cut on her forehead, was nothing by comparison. Maybe it was even the weather. She tended to feel shitty at the tail end of storms.

They had parked off the back side of the building and had to circle around the front to get to the main entrance. It made sense to go in the front anyway, since it was possible the police had stopped by without calling, to further examine Linzy's apartment or ask more questions. The guard at the front desk would know.

"Do you hear that?" Joanna asked as they turned the last corner before reaching the front doors. Linzy looked to her, inquiring without saying a word. "It sounds like . . ."

"A chainsaw," Linzy said, recognizing the sound again. That crew in the park must still be at it, maybe interrupted by the rain. "They've been cutting up fallen tree limbs since yesterday."

They were only a few steps from the front doors when they burst open, outward, in their direction. There was a buzzing sound in the air, but suddenly it sounded more like static. Overwhelming, crushing static in Linzy's ears.

All three of them gasped in shock.

Standing in the entrance was a man without a head. A man whose neck looked like a beet salad, with shredded red leaves around the perimeter. A man whose upper body was soaked in blood, which had cascaded and dried in trails from his shoulders and chest down his stomach, and in rivulets and spots decorating his exposed legs and feet.

He stood there for a moment of frozen time, like some powerful figure posing for a photo op, his legs spread in a wider-than-necessary base, his hands out to either side, holding the twin doors open.

He was naked. Mostly. The only article of clothing he wore was a collared shirt, open except for the second and third buttons, which remained closed, and caked in blood.

"Ohhh fuuuuuuccckkkkk," Joanna said, beating Carter to the punch. Carter said it anyway.

But they didn't realize. Not until Linzy spoke.

"That's him," she said. "*That's Ron.*" It was as if she tried to scream it, but the words were stifled in her throat.

How did he know they had arrived at just that moment? The man couldn't see. Could he somehow sense their presence, their movements? No, none of that made sense.

Had Ron's body been somehow hunting the apartment building all night, searching for Linzy? He—his body—was certainly standing there like some stalker, like some evil thing flaunting its power, on the verge of claiming some sick victory.

And that's when the sound of static in Linzy's ears changed back to the buzz of a chainsaw.

The blade appeared suddenly between Ron's legs, his limp penis and scrotum bobbing wildly as the moving teeth of the chain sped past, digging in, little bit by little bit. Soon, Ron's genitals were torn to bloody shreds, gobs of them splattering onto the pavement in front of, and below, where he stood.

The chainsaw blade continued moving upward, digging into Ron's lower abdomen first, spilling his intestines to the ground like a heap of wet rubber tubing before traveling up to burst the man's pancreas, stomach, and liver, sending splats of blood, bile, and other fluids in all directions. It took a minute to cut all the way through the chest, but the chainsaw made its way through the sternum with relative ease, as ribs cracked and Ron's heart tumbled out of his torso to the pavement below with a wet thud. Finally, the blade finished the job, breaking through the inner end of the left clavicle and exiting to the left of the spine, through the already ruined stump of Ron's neck, with a spray of crimson muck before disappearing again behind him. The two halves of Ron's body remained standing for a beat, lingering upright until the knees folded and both sides of the bisected body collapsed simultaneously.

The man with the chainsaw stepped forward and raised the machine over his shoulders. He, of course, was *also* without a head.

As were the dozens of men standing behind him, darkening the lobby.

If they'd had mouths, they surely would have all erupted in some sort of battle cry at that moment. Instead, the only sound Linzy, Carter, and Joanna heard beyond the buzzing of the saw was the stomping of a hundred feet as the Headless horde poured out of the building, their herky-jerky movements making the scene all the more uncanny.

FOURTEEN

Chase Matthews: And *News at Noon* continues . . . Our area saw some strange weather this morning, as a sudden rainstorm rolled in from the north-west. Gail Featherstone is off this afternoon, but Vivica Sanders is with us, and she has the story.

Vivica Sanders: That's right, Chase. What started as an unexpected passing shower turned out to be something a bit more unusual. *News at Noon* spoke with some area residents about an hour ago to get their reactions.

Shelby Haines (Local Resident): Well, I was out in my yard when the rain started coming down, and I noticed some of it sort of bouncing off the grass. I've lived here my whole life and never seen that.

Unidentified girl (7 years old): Gummies!

Bob Unger (Local Resident): Some kinda . . . I

guess I'd call it *soft hail*? Look at this. I mean, it looks a little like ice, but it's actually squishy, and it sort of jiggles a bit on its own. Never seen anything like it before. And it—*oh*!

Vivica Sanders: [quietly] Little bit of a rough edit there. [louder] Uh, moving into tonight's forecast, we should be clear, but don't be surprised if we see another pop-up shower or two. After all, we didn't see this one coming. Unfortunately this isn't an exact science, but we do our best. Back to you, Chase.

Chase Matthews: Soft hail, huh? That's different. Guess you really *do* learn something new every day. Speaking of things falling from the sky . . . In other news this afternoon, pieces of what authorities believe to be a communications satellite rained down earlier today in . . .

FIFTEEN

WE LIVE.
We hide in the rain.
We could have been bolder, but stealth was key, at least to begin with.
Now that we're here, it's important for you to know one thing:
We're going to take it all over—take you over—one by one.

SIXTEEN

NONE OF THEM WERE ENTIRELY sure how they had managed to escape the mass of Headless men, but they had. Fortunately none of them could move very fast, it seemed. Still, there was no sense in hanging around. None of them could predict what, or who, might be behind the next corner, literally or metaphorically.

Knowing what he did about the night before, Carter had to grab Linzy around the waist to pull her away from the scene and practically drag her along with him until she snapped back to life and started running on her own. Thankfully she was small enough and he could move her easily. He wasn't exactly musclebound, but he was big and had some power, even if he wasn't incredibly fast on his feet.

Joanna, not fully aware of what the plan was, had simply followed behind the two of them, hoping she wouldn't have any of the Headless too hot on her heels.

The entire city hadn't been overrun yet—at least they didn't think so—but enough of it had, in particular two of their three apartments, and probably the third soon enough.

But there was no plan. They just ran back to Carter's Accord, and he started driving.

Joanna was in the back seat again. She didn't mind. She was just happy to be relatively safe, happy these strangers had accepted her into their lives, as chaotic as they had suddenly become. While Carter and Linzy obviously didn't know each other incredibly well, they had some kind of history and lived in the same building. They were a little older than she was too. It was all enough to make Joanna feel like a bit of a third wheel, but again, she didn't mind too much. She could tell they were good people.

While Carter drove, Joanna and Linzy both sat quietly, texting people. Rather than sit in silence, he played some Plaid over the speakers. He was really in the mood to listen to Boards of Canada, but he wasn't sure how well that would fly with his companions. Not that BOC was particularly grating or abstract. He just thought of Plaid's melodies as being a little more accessible. He'd see how they went over. Maybe Boards would go on next.

Not that his choice of music was the most important thing right now.

Linzy messaged her mom, who lived in Phoenix now, as well as a handful of friends. Her mom had a habit of keeping strange hours, so it was no surprise when she didn't hear back from her right away.

She asked Sheinelle from work how things had been in her absence and if anything unusual had happened. A part of her still didn't believe everything she had seen since Ron came home the night before, and she felt a bit embarrassed that maybe she was in fact losing her mind, so she kept her texts with Sheinelle vague. Sheinelle told her they had all been sent home early, due to some emergency situation in the office building. The rumor mill had raised the idea of a bomb threat, but that's all Sheinelle had said. Linzy told her to stay safe.

She texted some other friends too, but the truth was, she felt as if she had let many—most—of her friendships slip over the past few years. The pandemic had certainly put a strain on everyone's lives a few years back, but Linzy had also gotten so wrapped up in her relationship with Ron and the idea of house-hunting and possibly even marriage, that she probably hadn't been the best friend to a lot of people.

Why had she done that? She lamented her actions and made a promise to herself that she'd fix this flaw whenever this whole crazy Headless mess ended. *If* it ended.

Joanna texted some people too. She had a few friends in the city—

people she knew from weekend nights at a queer bar downtown—but she wasn't terribly close to any of them.

She texted her therapist.

She had a brother she spoke to occasionally, but really only a few times a year. She texted him but didn't know if he'd respond. After all, it wasn't a holiday or either of their birthdays.

And she texted her old girlfriend, Kylie, from back home. They chatted occasionally. Kylie was a kind soul, and the one person from home with whom she remained in touch, other than her brother. They would text in fits and spurts, but Kylie was always wondering how Joanna's new life was going and seemed to want nothing but the best for her.

Joanna pressed the button on the side of her phone and the screen went black. She saw her reflection faintly in the glass, then decided to activate the camera in selfie mode to take a closer look at the cut on her forehead. It wasn't too bad. It had scabbed over and looked smaller than it felt. And if she positioned a few of her long curls a certain way, it was barely noticeable. Those few curls were stained red though.

They had finished all their water a while ago—four empty plastic bottles lay on the floor of the seat next to her—but she was able to squeeze a few drops out of one and use them to comb the stain out with her fingers.

She did still have a vague headache, but it wasn't the end of the world.

All things considered, she thought she looked pretty good. Pretty. And good. She snapped a selfie, getting the angle right on the first attempt. She wasn't vain, but she liked the way she looked. She thanked the genetic lottery for her high cheekbones. Most women would kill for a pair like hers.

You couldn't always have it all, but at least she had that.

"Not sure why I'm hungry again already," Linzy said. "We ate a ton at that diner."

But that had been a couple hours ago. They were partway through Pennsylvania at this point, with no real destination in mind. Carter had just decided to head west and see where it took them.

They had eaten Joanna's vegetable bounty a while back too, but, being mostly water, the cucumbers and tomatoes hadn't kept them very full for very long.

Carter said they'd probably need to stop for gas before too long.

His tank hadn't been full when they left town. They hadn't known they'd need it. Pretty soon they'd come across either a Wawa or a Sheetz, and in theory they'd be able to get food at either one. Unless wherever they stopped had been overrun by more Headless.

"In the meantime, there's some stuff in the glovebox," Carter offered.

Linzy opened the door and found an assortment of granola bars, trail mix packets, peanut butter crackers, and the like.

"Holy shit, dude, you've been holding out on us!" Linzy exclaimed. Her headache had faded and her mood, despite everything going on, had improved. She turned back to Joanna and offered her a choice of a few items, and Joanna took a small packet of chocolate-covered raisins.

"Sorry. Yeah, sometimes I feel a little faint in the middle of the day, so if I'm out, it's good to have some snacks around," Carter said.

"Faint, huh? Maybe that's something you should get checked out?"

"Yeah, I know. Maya used to nag me about going to the doctor all the time. My ex. That's probably why I've been resisting it."

Joanna didn't say anything. Her dad had been diabetic, way back when she still lived there, and there were days he really had a rough go of things. She wondered for a second how old he would be now, if he was even still alive. But surely her brother would've said something if he had died. Wouldn't he?

She checked her phone to see if any of her texts had been returned, but she had no signal. They were driving through the mountains now. Her phone would be fine again soon enough.

An alert popped up, reminding her she had to take her meds. She reached into her bag and fetched them, dry swallowing the pills, which she was able to manage, although she hated having to do it that way.

Her mind wandered as Carter continued to drive on. There weren't many cars out on this stretch of the highway, which could be a good sign or a bad one. A few raindrops hit the windshield.

"Do you think it's only men?" Joanna finally asked the others.

Neither Carter nor Linzy responded right away, as if they were each waiting for the other to do so. A moment later, Linzy turned partway back in her seat and looked at Joanna. She had a feeling she knew what Joanna was getting at.

"Well, there was that dog," Linzy said. "Might've been a girl. I didn't get a close enough look."

"Yeah. Maybe."

"I always assume all dogs are boys and all cats are girls," Carter chimed in. "But I'd be willing to believe I'm wrong about that."

The three of them all laughed as the car entered a tunnel. At the other end of it was a rest area.

SEVENTEEN

AFTER A BRIEF STOP, CARTER had continued to drive. His companions had both offered to take the wheel for a while to give him a break, but he'd been able to stretch at the rest stop and felt good to go for a while longer.

Eventually, however, he had hit a wall. And they had gotten low on gas again, after driving another five-plus hours.

Now the three of them sat, parked on the shoulder of a road, somewhere. None of them knew exactly where. It could've been western Pennsylvania still, or maybe Ohio, or even West Virginia. The GPS on Carter's phone had stopped working right some time ago and, to his embarrassment, he had completely forgotten to pay attention to the road signs in the physical world. He didn't take many extended trips, but when he did travel somewhere unfamiliar, he was so used to following the guidance of his phone, he often didn't absorb what was right in front of his face.

Linzy had fallen asleep shortly after eating her Impossible Whopper. And Joanna had seemingly been lost in thought for a while, then dozed off from time to time, lulled by the sounds of the road and the beautiful electronic melodies of Ulrich Schnauss, which Carter had switched over to after exhausting the Plaid catalog, or at least what he had of it stored on his phone.

Carter had been shocked, frankly—pleasantly shocked—the rest area had been open and the facilities were seemingly operating without any sort of recent incident, but he was more than happy to take advantage. He filled the car up with gas while the others ordered food, and they all took a moment to use the bathrooms. Back in the car, he was given the choice between a sad-looking Whopper and some even sadder-looking quote-unquote pizza. He had been hoping for a Wawa hoagie, but that hadn't been in the cards. And while he wasn't a fan of Sbarro, he opted for the pizza anyway because the idea of eating ground beef in that moment reminded him of Headless Ron getting halved by the Headless chainsaw guy, and his stomach turned at the sight of it. He chose not to offer his reasoning to Linzy.

Now, after having driven another five-hour span, he'd decided to pull off at the next exit he saw while the women slept. But, after a series of turns, he'd wound up somewhere on a long stretch of road with hundreds of tall pines on either side and not much else. Rather than waste more gas driving aimlessly, he had decided to simply pull over for a while.

He was tired. Three hours of sleep the night before, plus eight or nine hours of driving or whatever it had been, on top of *the fucking Headless apocalypse* or whatever the hell was going on? It was a lot. He needed a break.

It was getting dark, but it felt even later than it was, being tucked in the woods like they were. And the area was pretty desolate by the looks of things. Maybe that was good. No people.

He didn't know what their next move was going to be, but it was kind of nice to just sit and be quiet for a while.

He put the windows down for some fresh air, shut the car off, and leaned back against the headrest.

It was still so hot. It seemed like the summer might never end, and the feeling of dread that came with that was even stronger with everything they had experienced.

Linzy and Joanna both woke almost simultaneously, but they realized Carter needed some downtime, so they just sat quietly. They listened for voices, and for footsteps. They heard neither, thankfully—only an occasional gentle breeze in the trees.

Linzy poked her head out the window and looked up at the night sky. There were so many stars visible here. She wasn't used to that, living in the city, where so much of the sky's natural beauty was drowned out by light pollution. You could still witness some pretty dazzling sunsets from Joanna's neighborhood, but Linzy and Carter lived downtown, where they were more likely to see red lights blinking atop skyscrapers than stars.

The lights in the sky twinkled. She smiled at the sight at first, but then it struck her as sort of odd. They looked more like malfunctioning LEDs to her, blinking in and out at random intervals.

"What are we going to do?" Joanna whispered, her mouth right in the tiny space between Linzy's headrest and the door. "I mean, are hotels even safe, or do we just live in a car now?"

Linzy didn't have an immediate answer. They were just making it up as they went along.

To make matters worse, their phones weren't working properly. Either that, or they were in such a remote location mobile coverage was spotty at best. Maybe one of the recent storms had taken out a cell tower or something. But, of course, they had no way of knowing if the storms they'd had at home had even swung through this area. It was a safe bet, but not guaranteed.

There was no way to check. None of them had any sort of consistent signal. They might be able to access the internet for a few seconds, but as soon as they would enter a search, the browser would just spin. Same with the GPS. They could open a Maps app and see an image of the entire country, but their phones couldn't narrow things down any further.

Then again, their phones had been acting spotty hours earlier too. So maybe it wasn't just this region.

They had tried to text friends and family all day. It seemed like only half the messages went through, and none of them had received any answers.

They'd need to move again eventually, if for no other reason than to be somewhere with access to information.

"I suppose we'll have to re-enter civilization at some point," Carter said, reopening his eyes. It was no use. He couldn't sleep. Big surprise. He kept his voice down too. If there was anyone out there among the trees, they needed to stay quiet—which, upon reflection, seemed kind of crazy, given that these Headless people had no ears. "We're going to need gas again real soon."

"Wait," Linzy interrupted. "Do you hear that?"

The three of them went silent again and listened to the sound of a soft wind cascading through the pine needles. That part was nice. But buried in the ambient noise, somewhere in the distance, was another sound. It was metallic, kind of a dull sound, and somewhat consistent, but the rhythm was slightly off, and it seemed to stutter occasionally.

Kung . . . kung . . . k-dung-dung . . . kong . . . kung . . .

At the same time, a light tapping noise began too, all around them.

Tik . . . tik . . . tik . . . t-tik . . . t-tik . . .

More rain. Just a sprinkle. Carter turned his key halfway and put the windows most of the way up, leaving them all open just a crack, so they could continue to have some air and also try to determine what the metallic sound was and where it was coming from.

"Fuck, enough with this rain," Joanna said at full volume, exasperated with the toll the day was taking on all of them.

Linzy shushed her. "Quiet, Jo!"

Joanna glared at her.

"I'm sorry," Linzy said. "It's just . . ."

"It's Joanna. My name is *Joanna*."

"I know. I'm sorry," Linzy repeated, this time more seriously, meeting Joanna's eyes with her own. She felt bad.

Joanna nodded and turned her head to look out the window again.

Kung . . . k-dung . . . kong . . . kung . . .

Tik . . . t-tik . . . tik . . . tik . . . t-tik . . .

The rain stayed light, but the metallic noise seemed to be getting closer.

"What the fuck," Carter said under his breath. Then he turned to the women. "Do you see this?" he whispered, pointing to the windshield.

Among the raindrops, something else was landing on the glass. They could just barely see it in the hints of moonlight falling through the trees. There weren't many of them. Just a few. Tiny things, little specks that looked like those gobs of glue that sometimes kept fake cardboard credit cards attached to those so-called special offers that came in the mail. They were almost clear—translucent, really. They looked like maggots. Some of them landed and rolled all the way down the windshield. Others stuck.

"What is that?" asked Linzy. "Sap from the trees?"

"Weird," Joanna responded. Could this have anything to do with the flickering stars, she wondered, not sure why the thought even occurred to her.

Carter opened his door as quietly as he could and stepped out. He reached over the windshield and plucked one of the little things off the glass, between his thumb and forefinger. It really was like a maggot, but almost clear instead of white. It had tiny ridges along its length, like segments. And it wriggled between his fingers.

Linzy climbed over the center console and into the driver's seat to get a better look at what he had in his hand.

"It's *alive.* Like some little worm or something," Carter said. He thought back to Joanna's car accident earlier, when he found himself looking at the broken glass on the street, wondering why it seemed to be moving. It was raining then too. This was why. These little squirmy things.

"Well, leave it out there," Joanna said.

He squeezed the thing with the tips of his fingers, squishing it into two relatively equal halves before dropping the remnants to his feet. The thing left a slimy residue on his fingers, which he wiped on his hip.

Kong . . . kung . . . k-dung-dung . . .

Carter turned his head to the left as the metallic sound grew in volume. He had been so focused on the little maggot he'd lost track of the noise. Then, suddenly, he saw the source of it coming out of the dimness of the area, outlined faintly by the moonlight. There were two figures. First, a cow with no head, moving along at a reasonable speed, a clanging bell hanging from what remained of its neck. The strap attached to the bell appeared to be held in place by the angle at which it hung, and in part by a large flap of shredded hide, obviously thrown back by the explosive force of whatever had caused the animal's head to disappear.

A few paces behind the cow walked a man, tall and lean, in jeans and a shabby t-shirt. His hands and arms looked dirty, as did the knees of his pants. And he was muttering something.

"*Whoa Bethie . . . whoa Bethie . . .*"

It took a second for Carter to realize he was addressing the cow, presumedly with a lisp.

He checked. It was a bull. *A bull named Bessie?*

Neither the man nor the bull paid Carter or the women any attention. They simply continued on their path. As they walked by, Carter could see that a portion of the back of the man's head was missing. Not the whole thing, just his left ear and a baseball-sized chunk beneath it. A couple small gobs of brain matter sat upon his shoulder, and a trail of blood snaked down the back of his shirt. Perhaps whatever was causing heads to explode had been off-target with him. It had certainly gotten the bull though.

"Holy shit," Joanna said. "Fucking farmers, man." Linzy chuckled, but Joanna realized she had never told the other two about her experience with Mickey that morning. Then she thought of Gwyneth and wondered if she was okay. At best she was a widow now. She wished she had some way to contact her.

The rain began picking up, and Carter's shoulders were getting tapped by raindrops as well as the occasional worm.

"Why don't you get back in," Linzy said. "Seems like it's getting worse out there."

"Yeah, sure. Stay where you are, I'll go around." He paused a second. "Actually. . . Hand me my phone?"

Linzy detached the device from the dashboard mount and passed it to him.

Carter lit up his screen and activated the flashlight. He shined it over the windshield to examine the worms. There were a few more of them falling now. Most were hitting the glass and tumbling down.

As he turned to go around the car, he glanced down at his feet. Then he squatted and shined the light on the wet pavement. He saw the two halves of the worm he had squashed between his fingers, somehow still alive, squirming on the road. And in a flash, he realized what was happening. The halves were regenerating, each piece growing at an impressively fast rate, each of them becoming whole again. One becoming two.

He was reminded of planarians—the flatworms he, and probably everybody, had studied in elementary school. Using a scalpel, he and his fellow students had been instructed to cut the worms' bodies however they liked. Over time, each part of the worm would grow back fully formed. Two halves of one planarian would become two complete planarians.

Applying that memory to this moment, he became instantly more terrified than he already was.

EIGHTEEN

THE THREE OF THEM SAT in the car for close to another hour, windows up despite the heat, watching the sky get somehow even darker, listening to the sounds of raindrops and wormfall. The moon seemed to be obscured by clouds, but the stars above continued to twinkle in that strange way.

Carter was particularly quiet for a while, sitting in the passenger seat of his own car, until finally he had composed his thoughts.

"What if, like . . . what if those worm things are why this is all happening?"

Linzy and Joanna just stared at him in the darkness, listening to the tapping on the roof and windows of the car, waiting for him to continue.

"I mean, I don't know. I don't know what these things are, or where they came from. Seems like they're just raining down from the clouds, right? But, what if they're infecting people somehow? Like a parasite. Or some kind of sickness. Maybe they make people's brains swell or something. And then their heads go splat."

"This is some science-fiction shit," Joanna said, incredulous to all the day's events.

"I know it is. But how else do you explain people's heads exploding?"

"Sure, that's one thing," Linzy said. "But even if you have that part figured out—and I'm not saying you do—then how do you explain people continuing to walk around without their heads?"

The conversation didn't go much farther. They didn't have any answers. Just questions.

Soon, the rain subsided, and the stars regained their full brightness, solid in the way most people were used to seeing them.

They decided to move. They didn't know where they were going, but it was doing them no good to simply sit in the middle of nowhere. They would need to find gas somewhere, and they would need food again before too long. Maybe if they could get closer to another city they'd find a pocket of more reliable phone service and, along with it, some news.

Linzy started the car and began driving. She opened the windows partway so they didn't need to run the air.

Thirty minutes later, as the gas gauge was falling deep into Empty territory, Linzy spotted some signs. She held out hope they could make it to where they pointed. She willed the car to continue moving. Thankfully, they made it.

Crownview probably fell into the category of small town rather than small city, but it was good enough for them, as long as there was a gas station and somewhere they could get something to eat.

There were plenty of options as they rolled down what seemed to be the main street in town—a McDonald's, a Pizza Hut, Happy Dragon Chinese, the Crownview Diner. Being as late as it was, however, everything was closed. There weren't many lights on beyond a few streetlamps glowing yellow and traffic lights bathing their intersections in green and red, with occasional splashes of amber.

"Hey, I've got a signal!" Joanna exclaimed. Linzy jerked the wheel, startled. The glow from the screen illuminated Joanna's face in the rearview mirror.

Carter immediately reached into his pocket to see if his phone was working too.

"Ow, fuck," he said, extracting his hand, along with the device, from between his side and the door.

"What's wrong?" asked Linzy, startled a second time in the same minute.

"Nothing, just snagged my finger on something." Carter set his phone down in his lap and squeezed his fingertip, then leaned forward to open the glove compartment. He shuffled through the contents, much sparser now that they'd gone through his snack stash. The tiny light from inside illuminated his hand. "Just a hangnail. Fucking hurts though." Finally, he found what he was looking for. A Band-Aid.

"Got any more trail mix in there you haven't told us about?" Linzy said. Joanna suddenly looked up, anxious. They were all getting hungry again.

"Sorry. Just napkins and Band-Aids. You're welcome to nibble on one or the other if you like."

Carter finally glanced at his phone screen. He had a signal too, but it was weak. He had texted Maya from the diner, half a lifetime ago, but she hadn't responded. He wasn't surprised.

Joanna's eyes dropped back down to her phone. Sometimes it took a few minutes for things to refresh after a lost signal, but she would've expected that to have happened by now. Then, suddenly, her phone buzzed.

It was a message from Kylie, in response to one Joanna had sent hours earlier. They'd been having bad storms lately too, she said. She was dating someone new. And there was a serial killer in the news, but details were scarce, leading to all sorts of rumors, including one about the murderer cutting off the heads of their victims.

This caused a chill to run down Joanna's spine. She hoped the conclusion she was coming to wasn't actually the case, but it probably was.

She hadn't said anything to Kylie about the things she had experienced since waking up twenty-some hours ago. Not a word about the strange maggoty things falling from the sky, nor the headless bodies she had seen walking around attacking others, nor the fact she and a couple strangers she had met moments after crashing her car were now on an unexpected cross-country trip.

Maybe in a few days they'd make it out to Minneapolis, she thought for a second. It would be nice to see Kylie again. But no, if people were losing their heads out there too, maybe a visit wasn't such a good idea after all. Joanna liked her head right where it was, at the top of her neck.

Linzy pulled the car slowly into a gas station. The lights were on, dim and flickery, but there was no one in sight and it appeared to be closed. It was a few minutes after three in the morning, so this wasn't terribly surprising. She pulled over to the side of the lot, by an ancient, graffitied phone booth with no receiver, along the weathered brick side of the building that bordered the gas station.

"This place should open up in a couple hours," Linzy said. "You both okay with us camping out here 'til then?"

Joanna and Carter both agreed, and Linzy closed the windows most, but not all the way, then shut off the car. She was amazed they had made it. The car must have been running on fumes at the end.

"Cool. Why don't you two close your eyes for a bit and get some sleep then. Soon as this place opens, we'll fill up. Then maybe we can find some food somewhere and figure out what's next."

"Are you gonna sleep too?" Carter asked.

"Nah, I'm good. Might see if I can send a few texts and check some news from home."

Joanna realized she hadn't bothered to look for news. She got so wrapped up in finally hearing back from Kylie, she had forgotten. Of course, she was borderline delirious from lack of sleep too, not to mention all the rest of it.

But this sounded like a good plan. She'd let Linzy check for news. She slid over behind Linzy so Carter could tip his seat back, and she stuffed her mini backpack under her head like a pillow. The two of them were asleep in seconds.

Linzy listened to her companions' breathing for a moment before reaching for her phone. It was such a relaxing sound. She thought of Ron snoring lightly beside her in bed, something she would never get to experience again.

NINETEEN

Imani Desmond: Topping this morning's news, two more communications satellites are believed to have crashed to Earth in a stunning display. The country's top three telecommunications companies are reporting widespread outages in a variety of regions nationwide. But, in an unprecedented move, all three organizations have issued a joint statement promising services will be restored to full capacity as quickly as possible.

Customers noticed the disruptions yesterday afternoon, across the Southwestern US, as well as in Montana and North Dakota, parts of Ohio, Pennsylvania, and New Jersey, and most of Alabama and Georgia, but the joint statement was not released until late last night.

These videos, posted online by numerous individuals overnight, show what are believed to be pieces of debris falling to the surface—in a field in Oklahoma and into the Pacific Ocean—though how they were able to post said videos is still a mystery, given the outages. No injuries have been reported as a result of the fallen debris.

I know my phone's been on the blink. How about you, Brent?

Brent Wolf: Mine too, Imani. Now, let's take a look at another strange story, shall we? A man was decapitated in a tragic accident near the famed Pike Place Market in Seattle yesterday. While details of the accident remain scarce, one onlooker managed to capture this short video of the man continuing to walk, supposedly some twenty minutes after the accident. While the footage is blurry, and shot from quite a distance, you can easily see the man moving down one of the many piers in the area and over the edge, into the water below. Local police are asking anyone with more information about the incident to come forward.

Imani Desmond: And in yet another instance of the unusual, last night in Houston . . .

TWENTY

LINZY JOLTED AWAKE WITH A gasp. Her phone had just vibrated in her pocket. She had never even taken the thing out, her body instead deciding it knew what was best for her, sending her back into unconsciousness.

She had dreamt briefly of Ron. Of the two of them, in bed, him on top, pushing into her. She felt the pleasurable pressure of his erection filling her insides, more so than usual. The bed was cushy, like a cloud. She could feel him tensing, approaching orgasm. A few thrusts later, he grunted, pulling out, preparing to cum on her breasts. But where his penis should have been, there was a worm. A giant one, at least twelve or thirteen inches long, and thick like a can of spray paint. Ron leaned back, groaning as his orgasm erupted, sending half a dozen spurts of red fluid filled with tiny worms out the end of the larger one attached to him.

Thankfully, that's when Linzy had woken. It took a moment for her to shake the image from her mind.

She looked at Carter to her side, then turned back to see Joanna lying behind her. They were both still asleep, and it was still dark outside, except for the flickering of the gas station lights.

She pulled her phone out quietly to find she had a text from her friend Amber, who lived in Toronto.

R u ok?, it read. *Have u seen this? WTF! Hope ur safe!*

A YouTube link was attached.

The video's title, *What the F*@# is this?!?!?!?! LEAKED Raw footage Ch 12 News @ Noon*, was intriguing. *News at Noon* was something she hadn't watched since she was a kid. She wondered if the anchors were still the same ones she remembered.

She made sure the volume was down low and clicked.

It was, as the title suggested, raw footage from an interview with a local man. It wasn't in the city though. It had to be in the suburbs, somewhere, but it was a tight shot of a man, from the shoulders up, with nothing recognizable to Linzy in the background.

The man was probably in his mid-sixties, dressed in a white polo shirt with a blue baseball cap that featured a logo Linzy couldn't quite make out from the angle, though she figured it probably had something to do with a military branch.

Off camera, an interviewer prompted him, saying "Tell us what you've got there." The woman's voice sounded vaguely familiar to Linzy.

The man looked up to the interviewer, then down to his hand, which he held up, cupped from below. Then he looked at the camera, then back to the woman.

"Where should I look?" he said. "At you or the camera?"

"You can look at me," she replied. Her face wasn't visible in the footage, nor did the man address her by name.

"Okay. Wait, what do you want me to say?"

"Well, we're doing a story about the recent weather events we've been having. Just tell us about your experience with the rain this morning and what you've got in your hand."

"Oh, okay. Well, I mean, it was raining this morning, and I got up and said to my wife, ya know, if we don't get this dang roof fixed, we're gonna have bigger problems down the line. So we had breakfast and I went outside to get something from my truck, and that's when I noticed the rain was kinda funny. Some of it was, like, sorta bouncing off the driveway, and I thought, oh, it's not just rain—it's a hailstorm! But when I took a closer look, I realized it wasn't ice. It was this, I dunno, some kinda . . . I guess I'd call it soft hail? Look at this. I mean, it looks a little like ice, but it's actually squishy, and it sort of jiggles a bit on its own."

The camera zoomed in on what the man was holding. Linzy recognized it right away. It was about the size of a grain of rice. It was translucent, with several tiny ridges. And it squirmed in the palm of his hand. It was just like the stuff that had been hitting the windshield earlier. *Those worms.*

"Never seen anything like it before. And it—oh!"

The tiny worm leapt up from the man's hand. The camera, so tightly focused, wasn't able to follow the surprise movement, but the operator quickly pulled back and up to show the man coughing. He brought a hand to his mouth and seemed to struggle with a swallow, then he cleared his throat sharply.

"Oh shit! Are you okay?" the interviewer said with some urgency. She dropped the microphone she had been holding off-camera with a thud on the grass and rushed into the frame, placing a hand on the man's back, patting and rubbing it softly with the instinct of a mother. Linzy suddenly recognized her from her childhood. Gail something, maybe?

The man continued to hack and cough. He sputtered some half-words, but didn't seem to be in danger of choking. He was breathing.

The sound of the video was fainter and muffled from this point on, so Linzy bumped the volume on her phone up slightly, hoping not to wake her companions, who were still breathing deeply beside and behind her.

"Gosh," the man in the video finally said, his voice strained. "That dang thing up and jumped right down my throat! You see that?"

"I did. Here, take a drink." The woman grabbed a bottle of water from where she had been standing and unscrewed the cap, breaking the seal, then handed it to him. He sipped, then sipped again, then cleared his throat. His voice remained froggy. "Are you okay? Do you need to go to a hospital?"

"Oh, gosh no. I'll be fine."

"You sure? There's room in the van. We can take you right now if you want."

"No, no, I'm—" The man cleared his throat again. "I—"

Then Linzy spotted something. It was subtle at first, but she caught it right away. She wondered how many other people would notice what she did as quickly as she had. But she'd seen a lot in the last twenty-four hours. Too much.

The man's head appeared, however minutely, to be swelling. Looking closely, she could see the way his cheeks had begun to puff out at a strange angle, the way his jaw suddenly seemed uneven. And his face was beginning to turn purple.

"I—" the man said again, his voice slightly deeper, slightly muffled.

"Sir, I think you might be having some sort of allergic reaction," the woman said. She turned to look at the camera. "Joey, can you help?"

Joey set the camera down, still recording. In the frame was the grass of the man's lawn up close and, a little blurry in the near distance, three pairs of legs from the middles of their shins down. The woman was on the man's right, so Joey went to brace his left side. The man's legs buckled as soon as Joey reached him.

"I—" The man kept repeating the same word intermittently. "I—"

Then his body began to tense and convulse, as he struggled to keep his balance. The other two stayed right with him, seemingly helping to hold him upright. And then—

"Oh fuck!" Joey yelled. The woman screamed. There was a sound—a wet pop, like a water balloon bursting. Blood and chunks of brain and cranium rained down across the entire field of the camera's view. A drop of red hit the top of the lens and slowly crawled down the glass as the man's legs finally gave out. The interviewer and Joey let him fall this time, and his headless body crumpled to the ground, the ruined meat of his neck landing right in front of the camera. It looked like ground beef and strawberry jam with an eye of white vertebra at its center.

"What the fuck! What the fuck!" It was the same refrain from both people still standing. Pure panic. Pure fear.

"Let's go! Grab the camera!" the woman said. Joey snatched it from where it sat in the grass and the image abruptly cut to black.

Linzy sat there a moment, stunned by what she had just watched. She had already seen several heads explode today, but thankfully not as close-up as what she had just watched. If this was indeed real footage and not some prank or marketing gimmick for a movie designed to go viral, it was terrifying, and disgusting. She hoped that's all it was—that it had been fake. She'd be delighted to have been fooled. But she knew.

She scrubbed the video back to the moment the headless body landed in front of the camera—the autofocus took a second, but eventually it found the right depth—and she paused it. There, in the shredded stump of the man's neck, she could see them: several little pieces of a little worm—she assumed the same one—almost too minuscule to notice. But she did notice. She saw them there, within the wet mess of broken muscles and veins, each of them squirming, slowly growing. *Regenerating.*

TWENTY-ONE

***THE TIME HAS COME. OUR** time has come.*
But we must accelerate the process. We must reproduce at a faster pace. We must multiply.
Soon we will outnumber you. And as we take you down one by one, those of you who remain, however temporarily, must yield.
It won't be long now. We have found new places to be born. And to birth.

TWENTY-TWO

CARTER STIRRED. HIS EYES CRACKED open as he took a big breath in through his nose and peeled his forehead and cheek off the passenger side window. He had fogged up the glass but could nevertheless see right away it was still dark out, except for the lights illuminating the gas station.

"Oh *shit*, I'm sorry. I woke you, didn't I?" Linzy whispered, trying to make sure she didn't accidentally rouse two people.

"No. I mean . . . I don't know. What time is it?" His words were quiet and slurred from being newly conscious.

"Yeah, so about that . . ."

Carter made a face and stretched his eyes wider. "About that? What do you mean?"

"It's a little after nine," Linzy said.

"Nine? *Nine a.m.?* Why's it still dark?"

"That's what I'm saying," Linzy continued. "It still looks like night. And it's not storm clouds. Look, you can see the stars."

Carter leaned forward and peered through the front window, over toward the driver's side. Linzy was right. The sky was nearly black, except for the stars. He couldn't even see the moon.

"*What the hell?*"

"And on top of that, this town is apparently dead."

"*Dead?* You mean, like . . ." Carter wiped crumbs from his eyes. His bandaged finger still hurt.

"Well, not *dead*-dead," she said. "I mean, I don't know. Maybe. But I haven't seen a single soul. I figured this gas station would be open now at the very least."

"Have you tried the pumps? The lights have been on the whole time, right? Maybe the pumps are working."

"Shit, I didn't even think of that." Linzy picked her phone off the center console. "Here, take a look at this. I'll go check and see if we've been sitting here all night for no good reason."

Linzy pulled up the video again and handed the phone to Carter. Then she opened the car door, trying to minimize the creaking sound it made, and got out slowly. She glanced around to make sure there was no threat in the area. There didn't seem to be. The town was quiet aside from the hum of the electrical wires above and the air conditioning units keeping nearby buildings cool.

They still had working electricity here at least. She hadn't been sure if the lights over the gas station were flickering because of a power issue or just because the bulbs were going. Not that she had been concerned enough about it to get out of the car until now.

She reached the gas pumps and tried to operate them. But the screens were blank and the nozzles were locked up. Bust.

She took another moment to glance around the area. Up and down the street, nearly everything was dark except the streetlamps and traffic lights. A couple businesses had dim lights illuminating their storefronts but nothing seemed to be open.

Maybe this was just one of those towns that opened up late on the weekends. She had heard of places like this but, being a lifelong city person, she had never actually seen one.

Also, today was Thursday. At least, she thought it was.

Maybe something terrible had happened here. Maybe all the men had gone Headless and everyone else was either dead or too afraid to make their presence known. Like a ghost town, whether it was full of people hiding out or it had actually been abandoned. She felt uneasy standing there, thinking such thoughts. She decided to go back to the car.

When she got back behind the steering wheel, Carter was nearing the end of the video.

"*I—*"

"*Sir, I think you might be having some sort of allergic reaction . . .*"

Linzy eased into her seat and gently pulled the door closed with a click instead of a slam.

"I'm up," Joanna said, shifting her weight in the back seat. "Don't worry, you didn't wake me."

"Well, there's that, at least," Linzy said.

"What time is it?"

"You're not gonna believe this, but it's almost 9:30."

Joanna's eyes grew wide as she looked outside. "What? You fucking serious? *What the hell is happening*?"

"Wish I knew," Linzy said. "There's nothing going on, but I'm wondering if maybe we should all go for a walk, maybe see if there's some restaurant or store that's open, get some food. And maybe they can tell us when this gas station opens, or *if* it opens. Or if there's another one somewhere close by." She was trying to remain hopeful in spite of everything. Maybe it was just this section of town that was still asleep, or abandoned, or whatever. For all they knew, maybe things were happening a few blocks over.

Not that that would explain the dark. But it might be something.

"Good call. Yeah." Joanna repositioned her bag from under her head to her back, pulling the straps over her shoulders as she sat up. She smacked her lips. "Wouldn't say no to some toothpaste either."

Linzy turned to Carter. "You see the end?"

He bobbed his head once, solemnly, and scrubbed the video back about halfway.

"You might want to see this too, Joanna," Linzy said.

Joanna leaned forward to take a look at the phone in Carter's hand. Having watched the video several times herself already, Linzy looked back to observe Joanna's reaction. As she did, the look on Joanna's face very quickly turned to one of sheer terror.

But Joanna wasn't reacting to the video at all.

TWENTY-THREE

IT TOOK LINZY A MOMENT to figure out what was going on. The look of fear on Joanna's face was something she hadn't expected upon telling her she should check out the video on her phone. A bit of a wide-eyed expression, sure, but the level of absolute horror she saw reflected back at her was a surprise.

Then she connected the dots, and her own expression quickly mirrored Joanna's.

Linzy turned to look at the waning seconds of the video first, her phone held aloft in Carter's hand. But she realized Carter wasn't holding it at an angle Joanna could see from where she was sitting. Carter wasn't even watching it himself. In fact, he was barely holding onto the device, and a second later, the phone slipped from his fingers, falling to the floor of the car. The light from the screen created a strange moving spotlight effect as it cascaded downward, tumbling through the interior of the car before hitting the center console and then landing at Carter's feet, screen up.

Carter's face looked even more bizarre with the added lighting from beneath, and Linzy instantly saw why Joanna was wearing the expression she was. Carter's left ear was protruding at a bizarre angle, and the area at the base of his skull was swelling fast, as if a hose had been hooked up to his head, filling it with water.

Carter turned his head toward Linzy, and she saw the way the other side of his face looked, with his right eyebrow arched and swollen, the eye beneath it almost entirely exposed to the stuffy, largely recirculated air of the car's interior.

Even in the instant before she moved, she felt as though she could see the fear within him, as if he knew exactly what was about to happen.

"Go!" she screamed, and she and Joanna both scrambled quickly to open their respective doors and escape the confines of the vehicle. Linzy considered an attempt to grab her phone first but knew it could be a deadly mistake. Carter reached for her at the last second, but she was able to evade his grasp. She and Joanna both slammed their doors shut and Linzy squeezed the button on the key fob to engage all the locks. She wasn't sure it would keep Carter inside indefinitely—they had no idea how much humanity or how much ability remained in the Headless, not to mention the fact the windows were still cracked open—but it was the best she could do for the moment.

"*Tell . . . Maya . . .*" Carter said, his voice straining.

And then, just like that, he became one of the Headless, his skull exploding, bits of it tapping against the inside of each of the car's windows, blood and other goopy bits splattering everywhere, drenching the fabric of the seats, the plastic of the dashboard, the chrome accents.

The windshield and passenger side window took the brunt of the blast, but thankfully they remained intact. Some of Carter's gore spilled out through the sliver of space above the top of his window, like an overfull washing machine burping out suds. Then the car began heaving as Carter's headless body started to shake and convulse, the worm—*or worms?*—inside him learning as quickly as possible how to operate the organic machinery.

Would Carter's headless body, or the thing, or things, controlling it know how to get out of the car? Would it know to feel for the handle that opened the door? Did it have the strength and knowledge to smash a window? And how much time would it take for any of these things to come to fruition?

In the muck splattered against the inside of the driver's side window where she stood, Linzy thought she saw a tiny worm, or a piece of one, squirming and wriggling as it slid down the glass with the rest of the cascading slop, but she couldn't tell for certain. It didn't matter. She and Joanna needed to find somewhere else to be, immediately.

"Get back in the car! It's not safe out here!"

The voice came from a block away. A tall, skinny man, in long pants and an untucked short-sleeved dress shirt, was running under the dim streetlamps, seemingly for his life, his tie trailing behind his neck like a tail. He was barefoot too. Linzy and Joanna didn't know whether to run toward him or in the opposite direction. Each of them would help another human if they could, but any new person they encountered now could just as easily be a threat to their existence.

"I think I lost them!" he screamed, not quite as loudly, glancing over his shoulder in mid-stride. "Get in!" he screamed again, waving a hand at the two women.

Joanna and Linzy didn't go anywhere. Their feet were frozen. Their minds hadn't yet calculated what their next move was. The car beside them continued to rock irregularly.

It only took a moment for the man to traverse the block and reach the gas station. He finally slowed as he reached the opposite side of the lot, by the corner.

And that's when the other man—the very large, Headless one—erupted out of the gas station doors.

TWENTY-FOUR

Fiona Driscoll: . . . and meteorologist Kat Vasquez has today's forecast in just a few minutes, as well as a look ahead into next week, plus she'll talk to us about the various reports of so-called "soft hail" we've been seeing in our area.

But right now, we turn to this morning's *National Focus*. [fanfare plays] Reports are coming in, describing waves of unfathomable violence in a number of cities and towns all over the country. Yesterday, as well as through the night and early morning hours, hundreds of individuals, witnesses have claimed, have been continuing to walk, despite having been decapitated, and these headless individuals are—again, according to numerous witnesses—seemingly attacking other people.

It's difficult for us to fully understand the nature of what we're reporting here, and so far, we've been unable to independently verify some of these claims, but we feel it's in everyone's best interest to stay informed and safe, and it's important to share this information with our viewers.

Now, we'd like to caution you, if you have young children with you or are particularly sensitive to violent imagery yourself, you may want to leave the room or turn off your television now.

Unidentified man on video: Get away from me, man! Get the [bleep] away! [Bleep]! Are you people seeing this? Are you seeing this? I don't kno— Hey! I said get the [bleep] off me, man! Ahhh! Ahhhhhhhh! [man screams, sounds of liquid spraying]

Tyree Pendleton: And that's just one of several videos we've been reviewing this morning, this one in particular being something that was broadcast live on the apparent victim's social media feed late last night while attending a party.

We go now to Larry Boyega, our correspondent in Bailey's Notch, who's standing by with a witness to a similar attack that occurred locally early yesterday morning.

Larry Boyega: Thanks, Tyree. I'm here with, let's just say Walter, who has declined to give his real name. Now, Walter, I understand you witnessed something unusual yesterday morning.

Walter (Local Resident): That's right, Larry. And it's Henry, by the way. Uh, so like, I was with my lady yesterday morning, just trying to buy some corn from this farm stand . . .

TWENTY-FIVE

EVEN WITH HIS HEAD, THE man would've been an imposing figure. He was large enough that he had trouble passing through the entrance to the gas station without opening both of the side-by-side doors. And while his figure was large and round, it was easy to tell there was plenty of muscle beneath it all.

Without his head, despite having a little less mass, he was even more intimidating, and far more frightful to behold.

He burst out from behind the gas station doors like a jack-in-the-box.

Had he been in there the whole time? Linzy wondered. The idea made her sick, thinking about how close they might have been sitting to danger all night, not even realizing they could have been killed in their sleep. Not that it mattered much now.

"*Fuck,*" Joanna said under her breath. She reached out to touch her companion's arm. Beside them, the car continued to shake with the movements of Carter's rollicking Headless body. "Linzy, we need to go."

The larger man stood there, just outside the gas station doors, for a moment, as if he was surveying the area, looking for something. His body heaved with deep breaths, his lungs clearly still working somehow, which made no sense.

Not that anything made any sense anymore.

Then, quite suddenly, the beast of a man broke into a run, moving with a speed and agility perhaps no one would have expected. He made a beeline for the man in the tie, who had quickly stopped his own progress and tried to find the footing to send himself in another direction—a pointless endeavor. The larger man was on him in about two seconds, grabbing him by the shoulders, one enormous meathook on each. The thinner man tried to spin out of the larger one's clutches, but there was no use.

From there, the larger man slid one of his giant hands down onto the thinner man's left bicep, which he grasped onto firmly. And then he tugged. It only took two pulls. Two firm, violent pulls, and suddenly the smaller man's limb hung limply from his shoulder, the flesh torn, his arm still attached but not seated the way it should be.

He shrieked in pain, howling like some kind of wild animal. For a moment, Linzy thought the larger man was going to tear the limb off completely, but instead, he simply dislocated it and broke it partially away, creating a jagged seam where the man's chest met his shoulder. The larger man twisted the limb backward, opening the wound further and tearing the sleeve away from the rest of his shirt. The loop of fabric slid down his arm to his wrist, then past his hand and to the ground.

Linzy noticed the way the thinner man's hand was turned now, his palm facing outward, the fingers outstretched as if the arm itself was asking for assistance.

Then, something far more bizarre happened. Holding onto the smaller man, now with one hand wrapped around his neck, the other digging into the tear and pressing back on his damaged shoulder to open it wider, the larger man leaned forward, down to the same level as his victim, and aimed the wreck of his own shredded neck stump at the gash in the smaller man's torso. And with a heaving motion, the larger man's body vomited a torrent of blood from one wound to another, unleashing an unbelievable amount of liquid with the force of an open fire hydrant.

Even from where they were standing, Linzy could tell it wasn't just blood. Maybe being in the dark so long had enhanced her vision somehow, but she could see quite plainly: the deluge was filled with hundreds of tiny worms.

No. It wasn't her vision that had improved. *The worms were glowing now.*

TWENTY-SIX

WE ARE INVENTIVE. WE CAN *improvise. Even in our youth, we are more intelligent than your finest minds.*

We do love your minds though. We love your bodies. Their warmth. Their mobility.

Even in your simplicity, there are some things you can do that we, as young things, cannot yet.

But we learn. We grow. We adapt, in ways you could never imagine.

And we will do, and take, whatever we want.

TWENTY-SEVEN

JOANNA FINALLY CONVINCED LINZY TO move her legs, and they managed to slip away from the madness unfolding at the gas station without being noticed. They nearly ducked down an alley to make their escape at first, but it was dark, and they realized there might be someone, or something, hiding at the far end. It might have been the worst decision they ever made. How stupid would it have been, to have survived all the things they had so far, only to set foot into a dark alley like some cliche and be snuffed out by whatever menace was right there waiting for them?

So they stuck to larger streets. Ones with streetlamps. Ones where they could see who else might be around. Streets that exposed their threats.

A fifteen-minute walk from the gas station, they happened upon what was likely the real downtown area of Crownview. It was rather quaint, actually. Linzy probably would have liked strolling down the main drag, spending a day or two shopping, checking out a few restaurants with Ron. She imagined the two of them staying in a nicely furnished Airbnb for a weekend, just exploring the town. They hadn't gotten away in forever. But that would never happen now.

They spotted several Headless along the way, mostly sticking to the shadows. Some of them were walking casually, others were lying in corners, in some cases unmoving, and in others, twitching and jolting, trying to find their footing, so to speak. Joanna spotted one across the street from where they were now, elephant-walking on hands and feet, seemingly having trouble getting to a standing position, as if the legs were too slow to catch up to the hands.

They saw plenty of gore on the streets too—puddles of red filled with tiny islands of brains, skulls, and flesh. Even a few tufts of hair. And, of course, worms. Worms that were now glowing softly, with some blue-white bioluminescence. As if they had gained some new power. Or like they had all suddenly evolved.

Some of the worms wriggled in puddles of blood, while others were clearly able to move better, using a sort of twisting, drill-like motion that seemed to utilize their ridges like the threads of a screw to propel them forward.

Linzy and Joanna watched in horror as they saw worms crawl back inside the recently destroyed necks of the deceased. That seemed to be the way—or at least it was a good enough theory. The worms would find a way in and cause the head to explode. Then, if they had been expelled by the force of the explosion, they would simply crawl back in and begin piloting the body, like some kind of bizarre transport. And if the worms were injured in the explosion, no matter, because they were able to regenerate. Perhaps that was part of the process too. Maybe the explosions aided in their self-replication.

Maybe that's why some Headless got up and walked right away and it took others a while longer. But how long did it take to explode the head in the first place? Maybe there was no clear answer to that. Maybe they were wrong about all of this. But maybe not.

And if the worms could self-regenerate, how could they be destroyed? That was the most chilling thought of all.

Fire, maybe. But what were they going to do, walk around with matchbooks? Light one every time they saw one of these things and try to touch it with a tiny spark of flame? It wasn't like they could burn down every town and city these things had appeared in.

Another thought was: How had they been so lucky? It seemed like things were falling apart, people were being attacked left and right. And somehow, the worms hadn't gotten to them. Were they really just affecting men? They hadn't seen any women's heads explode—at least, not as far as they knew—but that didn't mean women weren't getting murdered.

They'd had some close calls, of course, and perhaps the calls were getting even closer, between Carter and the others at the gas station. But so far, so good. They'd do their best to keep their luck going.

But maybe all of this was wrong. Who knew?

Linzy and Joanna walked on. In some places, they witnessed worms crawling into cracks in the road, and into the spaces between the sidewalk pavers. That was new. Were the worms confused?

They passed what looked like a nice sushi place. Directly across the street was an Italian restaurant called Giuseppe's Trattoria. They paused a second to peruse the menu, and their stomachs groaned in unison.

"I don't know how much longer I can go without eating," Joanna said.

"I know," Linzy replied. "Same."

They walked slowly, zombielike, doing their best not to be noticed, down to the end of the block, then turned left. In the distance, maybe another block and a half away, they saw exactly what they needed. A supermarket.

They had thought perhaps they'd try to find a convenience store of some sort. If the gas station had remained vacant, they might have tried to break in at some point, thinking they would grab whatever they could, even if it was just Twinkies and trail mix. A convenience store would have been a little better. They might grab some bread, or yogurt, or cereal. A store like that would've had considerably better options.

But a supermarket was ideal. They'd have their pick of pretty much anything they could want, and in far greater quantities too. As long as the place hadn't already been picked clean by looters, they'd be fine. They just had to get in without incident, and then make sure the aisles weren't populated by the Headless.

It was a big place, set back from the street by a giant parking lot, all lit up brightly in the relative darkness of the town, like some oasis. The sign above the store read Moore Foods. It wasn't a name Linzy or Joanna were familiar with. Maybe it was a regional chain.

A handful of cars were scattered around the parking lot. In one of the corners by the entrance, there were construction vehicles, where a crew had apparently been working to repair a section of the pavement and install some sort of barrier in the form of concrete posts along the edge of the walkway that led to the entrance.

Their stomachs knew how close they were to nourishment, and they volleyed groans and squeals at each other like they were having a conversation.

"*Shut up,*" Linzy whispered to her own midsection. Joanna laughed silently.

As they got closer, the hum of the lights in the parking lot and the sounds of the supermarket's air conditioning system became more apparent. There was something else too. A sound, slightly high-pitched, like metal on rock.

Tink . . . tink . . . tink . . .

They located the source of the sound quickly. It was a man without a head, obviously a construction worker, raising a jackhammer—one that wasn't connected to its power source—with both hands, and dropping it, chisel first, into the ground manually, as if he wanted to break up the pavement but didn't understand how the tool really worked.

Linzy's head had begun throbbing again. And the sound of the jackhammer wasn't helping matters.

Off to the side, the construction worker's helmet lay on the ground, the opening turned up to the sky, filled with a small pool of red gunk. Even from a distance, Joanna could see a little glowing worm floating in the middle of it like it was enjoying a day at the pool.

Again and again, the worker brought down the jackhammer, driving its tip into the pavement, breaking up a small patch of the blacktop.

When the ground was sufficiently damaged, the man let the jackhammer fall off to the side and got down on his knees, at which point he leaned over and spewed a heap of blood-soaked worms out of his neck like a blast from a faucet. Down into the newly formed hole they went, their blue-white glow disappearing fast into the soft earth beneath the chunks of broken pavement.

And then the man stood up, grabbed the jackhammer, and moved further down the line, to break up more of the pavement. By the looks of things, he had already done this several times.

As Joanna and Linzy approached the supermarket entrance, they moved slower and more quietly, doing their best to remain undetected.

That's when they heard a voice. It was faint. Insulated. It was coming from inside the store.

"Help!" a woman screamed. "My baby!"

TWENTY-EIGHT

LINZY AND JOANNA LOOKED AT each other. Neither of them really wanted another test right now. They just needed to eat. They'd been running on nothing but adrenaline and fear for who knew how many hours at this point. It was dark outside and it still felt like the middle of the night, despite the fact that it had to be approaching eleven or maybe even noon by now. If they didn't find something to eat soon, they were both going to collapse.

They skulked their way around to the opposite end of the supermarket's facade, avoiding any notice by the construction worker, and thankfully not running into anyone else.

Linzy wondered how the Headless could sense others around them. Obviously they couldn't see anything. The worms must have some extra-sensory abilities, she figured. There was no other explanation, but then, starving and headachy, she wasn't thinking very clearly. And it all might be beyond comprehension anyway.

The automatic door peeled open as soon as Joanna set foot in front of the sensor. Linzy followed right behind, and they quickly ducked inside the store. The cool air was a blessing.

The coast seemed clear right off the bat, which was another

welcome development. Having to fight someone off or run in another direction the moment there was a bounty of food before them would have been the cruelest joke of all in a hilariously meanspirited day.

Linzy went straight for the produce section, which was directly in front of the entrance, and grabbed a green apple. She didn't care about the waxy coating, or the pesticide, or even the little oval-shaped sticker. She just bit in. Her eyes rolled back as she chewed and swallowed the first bite. This apple was the most delicious thing she had ever eaten. She devoured the rest of it with two hands, like a squirrel with an acorn, scanning her full field of vision the whole time, watching for unexpected threats.

Joanna had split off to the right instead, heading directly to the checkout area. She knew exactly what she wanted. Reese's Peanut Butter Cups. She dropped to her knees and slid right into the candy display, grabbing the orange package with one hand and using her teeth to tear it open. She was so hungry, she almost forgot to peel the brown paper cup off the chocolate. But she did and inserted the first piece into her mouth whole. Fuck apples. This was the stuff.

"My baby," came the voice again. It was a woman, sobbing. "Please help us . . ."

Joanna's eyes shot to Linzy, and Linzy returned the stare. They knew they had to scope out the situation, knew they had to help if they could. Linzy grabbed another apple, figuring if she couldn't eat it, she could always use it as a projectile weapon. Joanna stuffed the second peanut butter cup in her mouth and a handful of additional packages into her backpack. She threw a couple Snickers in too.

They moved halfway down the produce section, to the intersecting center aisle, then turned and began making their way horizontally across the store. Linzy took the left side of the center aisle, facing the back end of the store, while Joanna watched the right, which was the front half. They moved together, slowly enough to not make much noise, but fast enough they weren't wasting time.

"Help!" the woman called out again. They were getting closer.

It was crushing to see so much food on the shelves and not be able to dive in immediately. It was like a man forcing his dog to do a trick by balancing a treat on their nose, not allowing them to eat it until a specific command was given—cruelly drawing out the process tenfold.

Joanna's stomach gurgled. Linzy's replied.

They passed the canned foods aisle, and the one with soda and juice. They passed the aisle with all the snacks—chips, crackers, nuts, cheese puffs. Joanna's mouth was watering.

This place was huge. It had to serve the entire area—maybe not just this town. So how was it so deserted? Maybe the town *was* dead-dead. Linzy would've expected the shelves to be half bare, at least, from looting. Or, if nothing else, she figured the surviving population of the area would be here stocking up, whether they were paying customers or not. But it seemed they had the place mostly to themselves.

"Please . . ."

Well, not entirely.

They passed an aisle labeled *BBQ Essentials* and another emblazoned with a header that read *International Foods*. Then the woman called out again, and Linzy spotted her at last, down at the far end of the frozen foods aisle, toward the back of the store, where the meat cases were.

They turned left and headed directly for her, passing a full selection of frozen treats, from pizza to ice cream, on display behind foggy glass doors. Joanna's stomach growled again, like some kind of junk food detector. This was why she went to the gym.

The woman was standing right on the corner, half-tucked behind an endcap of ice cream cones, as if to keep hidden from any potential aggressors—or at least as hidden as possible. Her belly, full and round, protruded from the edge of the display. She was pregnant.

Like Linzy, she had dark, straight hair, but this woman's was longer. She wore a flower-print dress. The design was small and intricate, all red, black, and white. The fabric stretched, distorting the design a bit at the front of the woman's belly.

Her expression was one of fear and shock. She had to have been through a lot. Her eyes were both wide, though one was less so than the other. It appeared she might be blind in that one—or if not, maybe she had a cataract. Perhaps it was the lighting though. Fluorescent bulbs like the ones overhead and the shadows they created gave everything a not-quite-right look.

She appeared to have a bloody nose as well.

As Linzy and Joanna approached, the woman reached a hand out, welcoming their aid. Surely she was glad to see them, though her face seemed frozen in fear by whatever she had experienced. She stepped out from the corner, somewhat unsteady, and Joanna noticed she was barefoot. Not only that, but her feet, and what could be seen of her legs beneath the hem of her dress, were covered in blood, some of it dried, some seemingly half-coagulated, like jelly. There was blood on the linoleum floor beneath her too, and even more in a trail behind her.

"My baby," she said again. But, while Joanna heard the voice, she also noticed the woman's lips hadn't moved.

Linzy, being closer to the corner, noticed something else. There was a rope or something behind the woman, tugging at the back of her from beneath her dress, causing the skirt to rise up in a strange way. It was like a leash leading from her hips down to the floor.

Except, it wasn't a leash. It was an umbilical cord. And at the end of it was the woman's premature child, lying dead on the smeared tile, covered in blood and other fluids, and mottled with jellylike globs of red-black detritus.

There were worms too. They speckled the tiny body of the child, squirming around its belly and up along that end of the umbilical cord, glowing faintly under the fluorescent light.

Linzy gasped, and dropped the apple she was holding. The reaction startled Joanna, but she didn't need to ask about it. She saw the same thing a second later, as the woman took another uneven step forward.

"Help," the woman said again. But it wasn't the woman saying it. Not really.

They could see, now, the way her belly wriggled beneath her dress. The pattern may have made it difficult to notice at first, but it was obvious now. The bizarre, unnatural movements looked like something they had seen numerous times in the past twenty-four hours, and they braced themselves for an explosion.

Joanna and Linzy both had the same idea at the same time. They took a few steps back and moved to opposite sides of the aisle, each opening one of the many freezer doors and slipping themselves behind them, to use as shields against the impending explosion.

It all happened so quickly, but not the way they expected. The woman's belly continued to undulate and expand a few seconds more, finally stretching the front of her dress to its limit, splitting the fabric right down the middle, the two halves of the dress falling to either side of her body. But her body didn't break.

She wasn't wearing any underwear. Even in shadow, they could see the umbilical cord hanging out of the woman's vagina, slicked with red. A second later, it fell out of her to the tile below, like a wet rope, detached from within.

And a few seconds after that, the worms. The woman squatted down, her eyes still wide, her face slack, and they poured out of her vagina like a waterfall. Like a spigot turned to full blast. Blood, almost black, torrented out of her first, flooding the immediate area, spreading quickly across the floor. But that was merely a lubricant for the main payload, her womb's replacement cargo—thousands and thousands of tiny, glowing, maggot-sized worms.

So it wasn't just men, Linzy thought. Joanna began shaking violently, an uncontrollable nervous reaction. Both women stepped up inside the freezers, almost a foot off the ground, more than enough clearance over the shallow sea of worms and fluids flowing down the aisle.

"Now what?" yelled Joanna.

"Now we run!" Linzy called back.

They both dropped down from their perches, their sneakers squashing dozens of worms with each step. They had to move delicately. They couldn't afford to slip and fall in the river of muck. That would be the end of them for sure.

The woman's eye Linzy had assumed was blind turned out not to be after all. In fact, it wasn't even an eye. It was the tip of a worm, this one much larger than the others. It was thick like a kielbasa but much longer. The worm shot out of the woman's cranium like a rocket, finding purchase over Linzy's left shoulder, where it quickly snaked itself around her neck, tugging at her long hair, which pulled her head backward.

"No!" Joanna screamed. Panic struck fast. Now what? *Now what?*

Linzy reached for her neck, tried to grasp the tentacle-like thing encircling it and rip it away, but it was too slippery. She felt the ridges of its flesh and saw the way it glowed in her peripheral vision. At the very least, she needed to wedge her fingers in between the thing and her neck so she didn't get choked out, let alone strangled to death.

Joanna dashed back to her and tried to help. Neither of them could grasp the worm though. It was too strong and too slick. She had to do something. But what?

The worm pulled at Linzy, slowly reeling her in like a fish. She tried to keep her footing, but it was a struggle to do that and try to dislodge herself from the noose-like worm around her neck.

Joanna had both hands on the worm and one eye on Linzy, but she kept her other eye on the woman, fearful of what might come out of her next.

"Fuck!" she screamed at the top of her lungs.

And then, unable to do anything helpful, she ran.

TWENTY-NINE

WE ARE BORN.
We birth.
We multiply.
We feed.
We regenerate.
We fuse.
We grow.

THIRTY

JOANNA HAD DASHED OFF, BEYOND the end of the ever-widening puddle of worms.

Linzy battled with the thing around her neck, struggled to stay upright on the slippery tile. She gritted her teeth and pursed her lips together as tightly as she could as the end of the worm pressed against her cheek, seeming to want in. But she wasn't going down without a fight.

She was still tethered to the "pregnant" woman's eye socket, which she could see from the corner of her own eye as she twisted to keep her balance on the slick, slime-covered floor. The worm—what she could see of it, at least—had to be fifteen to twenty feet long, if not more.

Where had it all fit? Clearly it wasn't all inside the woman's skull. No, it had to have snaked its way through her body. But even so, where was there room? Maybe she'd been hollowed out, all her organs discarded or devoured. It was a sick thought. But plausible, perhaps, in this new hellish world.

The noose was tightening. She struggled to make as much space as she could with her fingers between the constricting worm and her neck, but it was getting more and more difficult as the seconds ticked by.

What if she doesn't come back? she thought. *What if Joanna abandoned me?*

It was a devastating, debilitating thought, but she couldn't blame her. This was living-nightmare, end-of-the-world type shit. If she had a chance to find a way out in the face of certain death, she'd take it herself. But still, she hoped.

There was a deep rumble in the distance. Thunder. More rain. Great.

But then, beautifully timed, Linzy heard the splashing, squishy steps of her friend's feet. She had returned with a few items in her hands. First up was a chef's knife. She tucked the rest of the items under one arm as she tried to open the packaging. But the blade was encased in plastic—the kind that couldn't be opened with one's bare hands. She needed something else, like a second knife, or scissors. She dropped the package and pulled something else out from the bundle she had pinched beneath her elbow. A pair of kitchen scissors. And thankfully, they were easy to open—a simple blister pack, a plastic bubble glued to some card stock. She thought about using them to open up the knife, but time was of the essence.

Linzy groaned, the pressure on her neck quickly becoming too much to bear, the force tilting her head to one side, slowly cutting off her circulation, not to mention her breath.

So Joanna did what she could and grabbed the worm's glowing length just beyond Linzy's neck. It was slick and nearly slipped from her grasp, but she wouldn't be denied. Then she hinged open the scissors and placed the crux of the blades on the sausage-sized thing and squeezed. The scissors slipped too, but she continued on, doing all she could to saw into the worm.

Finally, she heard the thing squeal and knew she was making progress. Its bioluminescence seemed to flicker slightly, like a dying light bulb. She kept at it, and at last, she cut all the way through the worm's girth. Clear liquid squirted from the wound, splashing onto Linzy's hair and shoulders, and coating Joanna's hands and arms. The longer portion, still hanging from the woman's face, fell to the ground with a splat. It flickered again, but the glow didn't stop entirely.

Linzy gasped, taking in more air than she'd had in several minutes. She ripped the smaller piece of the worm away from her neck and tossed it in the direction of the woman from which it had come. Then she hunched over and tried to regain her breath and composure.

But they were still standing in a pond of tiny worms. They had to go.

There was another distant rumble, this time louder, and surely closer. They felt the vibrations through the floor, the liquid at their feet rippling slightly. Another storm. This one sounded like it was going to be bad.

Joanna grabbed the package containing the knife from out of the slop on the floor and shook it once, hard, in a downward motion, to throw off whatever worms had crawled their way onto it.

"You good?" she said. "Let's go."

Linzy nodded. "Wherever we're going, let's find some towels on the way."

They ran to the end of the frozen section, where the center aisle intersected, where the worms hadn't reached yet, each of them debating internally which way to turn, or if they should just continue on straight ahead. But their movement stopped when they heard the voice of a child. It was a little boy, maybe four or five years old. Was it another trick the worms were playing?

"Mommy?" the boy said, inquisitively. This was immediately followed by a terrified scream. "Noooooooooo!"

THIRTY-ONE

Fiona Driscoll: . . . and unfortunately, this wave of attacks isn't restricted to the borders of the United States. In London, Tokyo, Sydney, Nairobi, Paris, Rio de Janeiro, Delhi, Mexico City, Karachi, Moscow, Shanghai, and elsewhere, there have been reports of people roaming the streets without heads—which is unbelievable enough—but to make matters worse, these headless bodies having been turning violent, attacking others in their paths.

In what may be a related matter, we're now seeing reports of concentrations of a so-far-unidentified type of small worm, in many cases measuring less than half an inch long, appearing in the same areas as these attacks. Some eyewitnesses have claimed the worms are somehow responsible for something related to the headless individuals, though whether it's the decapitations themselves or the reviving of the bodies is not immediately clear.

Also, some members of the scientific community have been getting vocal on social media in the last twelve hours or so, claiming that recent weather events in the same areas affected by these other incidents may also have a connection to the attacks.

It's a lot of information to process, and we don't have clear answers to everything just yet—it's an extremely fluid situation—but we're going to try to make sense of it as best we can.

I'm going to bring in Vincent Orr, our foreign affairs correspondent, who is standing by in Tokyo right now with the latest from that part of the world.

Vincent Orr: Thanks, Fiona. Uhh . . . Can you hear me?

Fiona Driscoll: We can hear you just fine.

Vincent Orr: Okay, well, we've traveled into Tokyo this morning from Kyoto. It seems the storms that ravaged Tokyo yesterday afternoon have, oddly, moved west to Kyoto now, and are intensifying, but we felt it was important to get to Tokyo and survey the aftermath.

We've encountered a number of Headless individuals so far today, but thankfully we've been able to keep a safe distance. We've also seen some of the worms that people have been talking about, and, as it's been mentioned previously, they do look somewhat like maggots. However, these worms seem to have some strange qualities, in that they are largely translucent. We spoke to one woman earlier, however, that told us she saw one of them crawl into her husband's ear early this morning, in their bed. She also mentioned the worm appeared to be glowing faintly, with a soft blue-white color. So far, we haven't heard that detail from anyone else, but there's a lot of neon here where we're standing in the Shinjuku section of the city, so we'll just have to wait to—*uggluk-gluk-guuuk* . . .

THIRTY-TWO

"MOMMY! NO!"

They stopped and looked back. It wasn't an illusion this time. The boy was real. His mouth was moving. And he was completely horrified—not to mention confused—by the thing his mother had become.

Did they really have to go back into that particular fray again?

The gory shell of the boy's mother was still in a squatted position, in the center of a massive pool of blood-soaked worms, her dress ripped open, her belly now somewhat deflated, and her other child, dead on the ground behind her, covered in tiny worms. A much larger one the size of a thick hose hung from the woman's left eye socket, stretching a good ten to twelve feet across the floor, convulsing periodically, splashing in the blood on the tile. Another, shorter piece of it was lying in the muck too, wriggling like a fish on the verge of death. It wasn't near death though. Both pieces of the worm seemed to be regenerating themselves, their forms glowing solidly again already.

Thinking ahead, Joanna took a moment to cut the chef's knife out of its plastic packaging with the scissors. She nudged Linzy and handed the blade to her.

"Hey kid!" Linzy yelled. "It's not safe here. Run down the next aisle and we'll meet you, okay?" She motioned to her right, his left.

The boy looked down the frozen foods aisle at the women but didn't respond to them.

"Mommy? What's happening?"

The woman, the husk of the boy's mother, stood up slowly and turned sideways to face her son. He gazed up into her remaining eye, which was still open wide, but he couldn't tell if it was looking back at him.

More thunder sounded outside. The seals on the freezer doors crackled.

"Honey, that's not your mommy anymore, okay? I know this doesn't make sense, but we need to get you out of here quickly."

Linzy considered running back down the aisle, thinking she could somehow scoop the boy up and run away, but she thought twice about it, fearing for her own safety. If she couldn't guarantee it for herself, how could she help anyone else?

"Please, just come down the next aisle over and we'll get you somewhere safe."

Linzy and Joanna watched as the giant worm pulled back, slowly retracting into the woman's body, via her face, with a dull slurp.

"Come on, kid, *please*!" Joanna yelled, joining her friend's plea. "We'll help you!"

Then the woman's head tilted back, slowly, and her lips parted. When her jaw began to lower, Joanna and Linzy knew what was about to happen. They screamed wildly for the boy to run.

A giant worm—possibly the other end of the one that had attacked Linzy—shot out from between the woman's teeth.

The boy moved to his left with impeccable timing, whether he had intended to avoid the projectile or not.

"Mommy!" he screamed again and began crying. Then, finally, to the relief of Joanna and Linzy, he ran.

The women dashed down the center aisle, over to the next numbered aisle to greet him. But he had already run past that one.

"Shit," Joanna said.

They ran to the next aisle, but just as they arrived, a Headless man turned the corner, surprising them, his arms raised as if in search of a hug. Thunder rumbled outside, as if to punctuate the man's appearance, like some old black-and-white horror film.

Linzy managed to duck beneath his reach, and Joanna was able to stop short. Clearly sensing their presence, he swiped with both arms, knocking a box of trash bags off the endcap in the process.

Not knowing what else to do, Joanna gripped the handles of her closed scissors tight and swung at him with a backhand motion. The twin blades sank right into the center of the man's chest, breaking through the breastplate. She had no way of knowing for sure, but she hoped she had pierced his heart.

She held the scissors there for a second as the man froze in place, then ripped them out with as much force as she had thrown them in. A spurt of blood escaped the man's chest, and he dropped to his knees. Joanna took several steps back as he fell forward and a wave of worms and blood sprayed out from his neck.

Joanna was quick to move out of the way, jumping over the encroaching puddle, and past the body to join Linzy on the other side of the intersection of aisles. As she moved, a few of her curls swung in front of her face, and she could see one of them was stained red again.

Linzy gaped at the sight of the fallen body.

"Is that it?" Linzy said. "Is that the key?" Joanna looked at her. Linzy was thrilled. "We need to stab their hearts! That's it!"

Joanna wasn't as excited or hopeful. True, the act may have downed one man, but it didn't seem to kill off the worms. Surely there were still some inside his body, but plenty had escaped through his neck and they were moving just fine across the wet linoleum.

"Let's go," she said. "The boy."

They continued down the center aisle, but before they had gotten to the next numbered row, they saw the boy cross the center at the far end of the store. He was moving toward the front.

Linzy called to him, but he didn't reappear. It made sense. There was madness all around. The boy's mother—or rather, the thing inside her body—had just tried to attack him. And she and Joanna were strangers. What do all good mothers tell their children about people they don't know? *Of course* he was going to avoid them.

They continued to move in his direction anyway, turning right, down the next aisle they came to, which led to the front of the store. Maybe they'd rendezvous with him there, by the registers, if they didn't run into any more obstacles along the way.

Halfway down the aisle, the building shook. It was loud—much louder than the rumbles they had been hearing so far. Joanna lost her footing in mid-stride and fell to the floor. Linzy skidded to a stop and backtracked to help her up.

Was that more thunder, or was it an earthquake? *How much more would they have to face?*

They made their way to the row of registers at the front of the store. Joanna scanned the right side of the space for the boy, while Linzy scoured the left. He was nowhere to be found.

"Little boy?" Linzy called out. "Listen, we're here to help. We want to take you somewhere safe. Can you come out for us?"

"Uggh! Linzy!"

A Headless man wearing one of the store's cashier aprons had surprised Joanna, stepping out from who knows where and grabbing her from behind, both arms wrapped around her waist like a seatbelt. Oddly enough, her first thought was that he was going to smash the peanut butter cups in her bag.

She struggled, clawing at his arms with one hand and using the scissors with the other, in an attempt to pry his arms off, trying to break his hold. The way she was being held, she had no opportunity to stab him in the chest.

"Fuck!" Linzy screamed as she turned to see her friend in trouble. She bolted right for her and circled around behind the Headless guy on her back. She debated stabbing him but didn't want to hit some random part of the body she knew would do no good, nor did she want to accidentally hurt Joanna in the process. Instead she tugged at the man's shoulders, trying to peel him off Joanna. But he was far too strong.

"Okay, I'm gonna try something," she said, grasping the knife in her hand firmly. "When I say so, lean forward as far as you can!"

"Got it. Just hurry!"

"Ready? Now!"

Joanna lurched forward, and Linzy stabbed the man, right in the middle of the back—just left of center, enough to miss the spine. Only the tip of the blade went in, though, when she hit some resistance. *Ribs.* She hit his ribs.

"Stay forward," she said. "Going again." She turned the knife ninety degrees with her hand, so the blade would be horizontal this time upon impact, and slammed it in with everything she had. She felt something hard inside and figured she had glanced off another rib, but the blade went in much deeper with this blow. She used her other hand to press the end of the handle in as far as it would go. The man's body tensed, then loosened. His arms released their might and Joanna broke free. Linzy extracted the blade and stepped out of the way, as blood and worms sprayed out from the wound in his back and the stump of his neck. The women moved quickly to avoid the spill.

"Thank you," Joanna said through a sigh of relief.

"Look! Hey!" It was the boy, skating through one of the register lanes. Before they knew it, he was gone, out the automated exit door.

They looked around to make sure no more Headless were about to surprise them, then darted toward the front.

Through the windows, the sky outside looked even darker than it had before. Maybe it was, or maybe it was a simple trick of the light inside that made the outside look that way.

There was another rumble of thunder that felt very close, but it didn't appear to be raining. And there was no lightning at all.

"Over there!" Joanna said, pointing out the boy. He was running though the parking lot. They quickly exited through the same door he had. When they got outside, though, it was a totally different situation than they had expected.

THIRTY-THREE

DOZENS OF HEADLESS WERE MILLING about the parking lot, scattered all across it, as if each of them had their own small tract of land to maintain and defend.

But the lot itself may have been the strangest-looking thing of all. When they had made their way into the supermarket, the only thing out of the ordinary Linzy and Joanna had seen in the area—all things being relative, of course—was the lone Headless construction worker hacking away at the pavement with a jackhammer. Now, however, there were deep trenches carved through the surface, from one side of the parking lot to the other, chunks of broken asphalt lying in massive piles along the edges. And half the cars that had been sitting in the lot before had been overturned.

There was no way the construction guy could have done all that. Not with the jackhammer—not even if he had been using it the proper way. Unless . . . Had he somehow operated one of those larger pieces of machinery? The backhoe? Was that the rumbling they'd been hearing from inside the store?

They got their answer a minute later, as one end of a giant worm—one ten times larger than the one inside the boy's mother—tore across the lot like a shark fin, breaking up the blacktop like some kind of industrial-strength plow, knocking over another car in the process too. Its spiraled ridges twisted as it moved, as if the worm was spinning, drilling its way through anything in its path.

Was this happening everywhere? Or just here, like the two of them were some essential target?

The worms were getting so much bigger now. *Were they feeding on something?*

"There he is!" On the left side of the lot, Joanna spotted the boy. He was running where he could across the parts of the lot that remained flat, and climbing over the heaps of rocky, broken pavement with the skill and dexterity of a child several years older.

"How are we going to get to him?" Linzy asked. Joanna just stared, shaking her head faintly.

The boy leaped over the tilled portions—the valleys—with relative ease and managed to avoid any of the giant worms now racing back and forth across the lot, breaking up more and more of it with each pass.

But where did he think he was going?

They had their answer soon enough.

The boy ran right into the arms of one of the Headless.

The man was wearing a tropical shirt, turquoise and white, with accents of yellow surfboards riding the stylized waves of the design in between the trails of blood also decorating the man's chest. He grabbed the boy's shoulders with his hands, almost affectionately, and held him there in place, not doing anything else. The boy scanned him from waist to shoulders, looking up to where the man's head should have been. Then the man moved his hands under the boy's armpits and raised him up into the air, so they would have been face to face, if he'd still had a face.

"That's my daddy's shirt," the boy said, confused.

Then three more Headless men came out of the shadows, each from a different direction. They moved more steadily than the ones Joanna and Linzy had seen only an hour or two earlier. Maybe the worms had gotten more skilled in their handling of the equipment.

The Headless moved in toward the boy, who was still being held aloft by the man in the tropical shirt, until finally he was surrounded on all sides. The one standing directly behind him grabbed the boy's t-shirt by the back of the collar and yanked downward, tearing the garment right off him in a swift motion. Then the three of them turned their backs to the boy and dropped down into crabwalk positions, supporting themselves with hands and feet, their backs facing the ground, their chests pointing up to the sky.

Joanna and Linzy could only stare at the display, confused and horrified.

The man in the tropical shirt lowered the boy back to the ground as the other three inched closer to him, their bloody, shredded necks closing in like the foaming mouths of hungry beasts.

Then they pressed their necks against the boy's abdomen. And he screamed.

Linzy and Joanna couldn't see exactly what was happening, or comprehend the mechanics of it, but they knew it was bad. The boy howled like he was being burned.

The tropical-shirted man let go of the boy as soon as the other three had him, and he turned around himself, to drop down like the others had, before pushing his neck up against the remaining open section of the boy's midsection.

Again the boy screamed. Whatever they were doing looked excruciating. But it was all over soon enough, as the screams stopped and the boy's face went blank, and his head tipped forward.

The four Headless men and the boy were one body now, fused together by some method unknown to humankind. Linzy and Joanna couldn't even scream in terror at what they had just witnessed. They just stood there, gaping, defeated, as the hideous thing skittered off in the opposite direction.

The monstrosity moved as a single spiderlike creature now, seemingly so much faster and more agile than any of its components had been on their own before. The women watched as it traversed the ruined parking lot, climbing expertly over the heaps of broken pavement and jumping over the gaps between them with ease. It was an oddly beautiful thing in its own demented way. A new use for flesh. Bodies made more efficient.

The ground shook again as another giant worm forged a path across the parking lot, but the women barely noticed as they watched the obscene spider-thing cross the street. It began scaling the side of a building there, smashing each corner window with its arms and legs as it climbed higher and higher.

THIRTY-FOUR

THE TIME HAS ALMOST COME.

Did you think we were everything?

No. We are but the first wave. We are merely the preparation.

To those of you who remain, for now, prepare yourselves. For you are about to witness true majesty. Your new god arrives. Bow down.

THIRTY-FIVE

TikTok Voiceover: I mean, just look at some of this footage showing up online. Two Headless bodies fused at the necks, cartwheeling down the road like a couple of conjoined acrobats? This crabby thing, where it looks like four men attached to a child? Look how fast that thing is moving! What about this zookeeper who seems to have attached his neck to a tiger's . . . err, hindquarters? It's madness!

Look at this one! A row of six men, all Headless, all joined at the shoulders where their arms were removed, walking in a line! I mean, they look like a chain of paper dolls or something!

And this giant worm thing that's impaled this poor woman like that scene in *Cannibal Holocaust*! But it's just skating around, crashing into buildings, knocking down everything in its path. Unbelievable!

Local police forces aren't enough to tackle this. *Where's the military? Where's the National Guard? Where is our government?*

THIRTY-SIX

"THIS IS NEVER GOING TO end," Joanna said.

The spider-thing had run off moments ago, but there were other abominable creatures making their presence known. One in particular seemed especially incomprehensible: One Headless man had ripped the arms and legs off another, and then five more Headless had fused their necks to the wounds of that torso. From there, more arms and legs had been removed and more bodies had attached themselves. Linzy and Joanna watched the process from in front of the supermarket in a state of bewilderment. It only took a few minutes.

The end result was a sort of dome, formed from a latticework of bodies, like a schoolyard jungle gym, but much larger. And the thing moved too, by tensing its musculature and inverting its domelike shape, flipping its structure forward. It reminded Linzy vaguely of a Slinky, the way that toy could be made to cascade down stairs. But this was entirely its own horrid thing, so bizarre and alien Linzy would barely have been able to describe it to someone if she had been asked.

"I don't think we have much time left, Linz."

"Hey. *My name is Linzy.*" She elbowed Joanna lovingly. They both smiled, or at least did their best.

"Seriously though. Even if we could stab every man on the planet in the heart—and how could we coordinate that? But even if we could, so what? The worms are still alive. And they're inhabiting women now too. This isn't a men and women thing. Shit, they don't even need bodies, really. They're in the ground too!"

A giant worm sailed right past them at that moment, spinning, shaking the ground, carving a fresh path through the blacktop of the parking lot, right where it met the curb in front of the supermarket's entrance. They nearly lost their footing.

The body of a woman was atop the worm, its tip thick like a jar of mayonnaise, hanging out of her mouth like a swollen, glowing tongue. The rest of the worm, even larger, snaked out of her lower half, her body spinning limply on its twisting ridges. Thankfully her skirt hid where exactly she had been penetrated, but both of her legs and her shoes were slicked solid red.

It was getting to the point where things like this didn't even faze them anymore.

"So what then?" Linzy asked.

"These were in the same aisle as the scissors," Joanna said, reaching into the back pocket of her cutoffs and extracting a box of matches. "I think we have to burn it all down."

It took a second for Linzy to comprehend what Joanna was saying.

"*What?* Burn it all—? *What are you talking about?*"

"Look, fire kills everything, right? That's the only solution I can think of." Joanna was dead serious. Killing the human bodies they inhabited didn't kill the worms. Chopping the worms up only made more of them. As far as she saw things, they were out of options.

"What, we *scorch the earth*? Live out the rest of our days in a charred wasteland? I don't know, babe." Linzy still held out hope for some miraculous solution, some savior to come along and fix everything, even if it was at the eleventh hour. And it felt like it was almost midnight.

The sky was the darkest it had been yet. It looked like literal midnight, despite it surely being afternoon at this point. The clouds overhead looked like thick, black smoke, and they seemed to be swirling, almost like a whirlpool in the sky.

"I'm thinking we head back to the gas station. Maybe the coast is clear now. And if so, we can figure out a way to break into the pumps, spread some gas around, light things up."

It was certainly an idea. But was it a *good* one? Linzy couldn't reconcile it. She paused a moment and thought of Ron again, wondered where the worm, or worms, that had been inside him were now. She hadn't had a chance to grieve yet, not really. And she certainly hadn't fully come to grips with how close she had come to her own end that night.

The two of them continued to gaze at the scene playing out before them. What was their next move?

Linzy wasn't sure she wanted to be a part of Joanna's plan. But she didn't want them to go their separate ways either. *What was she going to do?* She couldn't decide.

She looked up at the spiraling clouds again, watched them swirl their inky blackness directly overhead. It was the darkest dark she had ever seen. But then, suddenly, at the center of this particular mass, there seemed to be a break. An opening. A hint of light. *At the end of the tunnel?*

The clouds slowly began to part. And yes, some light was breaking through. Maybe this was the miracle she'd been hoping for. Or maybe just—

"Oh shit," Linzy said. "Look! *The moon!*"

Joanna saw it too. The whirlpool of clouds opened at its center, a tiny dot of light appearing there. The glowing orb in the center of the black illuminated the sky ever so slightly at first, then more as it gradually expanded, growing larger and larger, casting its majestic light down to the ground below.

She stood there for a moment in awe of the sight. It was beautiful to behold. But it wasn't the moon. The moon didn't look like that, didn't have that kind of opening on the end. The moon didn't grow like that either. And it never, not even in movies, looked quite so large in the sky as it did now.

There was a metallic sound at her feet, the clatter of steel on stone. At the same moment a glint of light had flashed in the corner of her eye. The sound seemed familiar, jarring her out of the moment she was experiencing. She glanced down to the pavement beneath their feet and saw what made the noise. It was a knife. *The chef's knife she had given to Linzy.* She had dropped it.

Then she looked up to Linzy's face and saw why. It had gone slack. Her nose was bleeding, a red trail rolling over her lips, down to and off her chin, dripping onto her top. And her eyes had gone wide and blank.

No, Linzy. *No.*

Her face began to distort, to stretch, if only slightly at first. But Joanna could see it plainly. She watched in horror as Linzy's throat bulged, then her cheeks pulled taut as her head tipped back. Her lips parted slowly, and her jaw opened as more blood dripped off her chin. Connective tissue popped, and the corners of her mouth began to split, her cheeks tearing as more blood cascaded down the lower half of her face, and the tip of an enormous glowing worm started working its way out, peeking over the back of her tongue.

"You were wrong," the worm said, using Linzy's voice, but not her lips. It startled Joanna, and she shuddered at the sound. "Things *do* end. And other things *begin.*"

Joanna had no words. Just a feeling of utter defeat. Deep down, she knew this was inevitable.

Her headache had disappeared for some time, but suddenly she became aware of it again.

She looked back up to the clouds, at the ever-widening circle in the sky—the portal through which the largest worm she had seen yet, glowing brightly, was making its entrance into their world.

Although it wasn't their world any longer.

She thought of Gwyneth back at the farm stand again and wondered how she was doing. If she was okay. If she was still alive. If her body had been taken over yet. She had always been so nice to her.

Then she felt dampness on her upper lip and realized her own nose had begun to bleed. The box of matches slipped from her hand, but she didn't even hear it hit the ground. All she heard was static, her head throbbing with the fuzzy sound of it. Her eyes pulsated. Her throat felt swollen, felt . . . clogged. Was she even breathing anymore? She wanted to scream but couldn't operate her vocal cords. She couldn't move. Her entire body began to tingle. Her jaw hurt. And then, against her will, it opened steadily, wider than it should. And her cheekbones, which she had always been so proud of, slowly began to crack.

Scott Cole is a writer, artist, and graphic designer living in Philadelphia. Find him on social media, behind you in the mirror, or at 13visions.com.

Other Grindhouse Press Titles

#666__*Satanic Summer* by Andersen Prunty
#099__*The Killing Kind* by Bryan Smith
#098__*An Affinity for Formaldehyde* by Chloe Spencer
#097__*Kill The Hunter* by Bryan Smith
#096__*The Gauntlet* by Bryan Smith
#095__*Bad Movie Night* by Patrick Lacey
#094__*Hysteria: Lolly & Lady Vanity* by Ali Seay
#093__*The Prettiest Girl in the Grave* by Kristopher Triana
#092__*Dead End House* by Bryan Smith
#091__*Graffiti Tombs* by Matt Serafini
#090__*The Hands of Onan* by Chris DiLeo
#089__*Burning Down the Night* by Bryan Smith
#088__*Kill Hill Carnage* by Tim Meyer
#087__*Meat Photo* by Andersen Prunty and C.V. Hunt
#086__*Dreaditation* by Andersen Prunty
#085__*The Unseen II* by Bryan Smith
#084__*Waif* by Samantha Kolesnik
#083__*Racing with the Devil* by Bryan Smith
#082__*Bodies Wrapped in Plastic and Other Items of Interest* by Andersen Prunty
#081__*The Next Time You See Me I'll Probably Be Dead* by C.V. Hunt
#080__*The Unseen* by Bryan Smith
#079__*The Late Night Horror Show* by Bryan Smith
#078__*Birth of a Monster* by A.S. Coomer
#077__*Invitation to Death* by Bryan Smith
#076__*Paradise Club* by Tim Meyer
#075__*Mage of the Hellmouth* by John Wayne Comunale
#074__*The Rotting Within* by Matt Kurtz
#073__*Go Down Hard* by Ali Seay
#072__*Girl of Prey* by Pete Risley
#071__*Gone to See the River Man* by Kristopher Triana
#070__*Horrorama* edited by C.V. Hunt
#069__*Depraved 4* by Bryan Smith
#068__*Worst Laid Plans: An Anthology of Vacation Horror* edited by Samantha Kolesnik
#067__*Deathtripping: Collected Horror Stories* by Andersen Prunty
#066__*Depraved* by Bryan Smith
#065__*Crazytimes* by Scott Cole

#064__*Blood Relations* by Kristopher Triana
#063__*The Perfectly Fine House* by Stephen Kozeniewski and Wile E. Young
#062__*Savage Mountain* by John Quick
#061__*Cocksucker* by Lucas Milliron
#060__*Luciferin* by J. Peter W.
#059__*The Fucking Zombie Apocalypse* by Bryan Smith
#058__*True Crime* by Samantha Kolesnik
#057__*The Cycle* by John Wayne Comunale
#056__*A Voice So Soft* by Patrick Lacey
#055__*Merciless* by Bryan Smith
#054__*The Long Shadows of October* by Kristopher Triana
#053__*House of Blood* by Bryan Smith
#052__*The Freakshow* by Bryan Smith
#051__*Dirty Rotten Hippies and Other Stories* by Bryan Smith
#050__*Rites of Extinction* by Matt Serafini
#049__*Saint Sadist* by Lucas Mangum
#048__*Neon Dies at Dawn* by Andersen Prunty
#047__*Halloween Fiend* by C.V. Hunt
#046__*Limbs: A Love Story* by Tim Meyer
#045__*As Seen On T.V.* by John Wayne Comunale
#044__*Where Stars Won't Shine* by Patrick Lacey
#043__*Kinfolk* by Matt Kurtz
#042__*Kill For Satan!* by Bryan Smith
#041__*Dead Stripper Storage* by Bryan Smith
#040__*Triple Axe* by Scott Cole
#039__*Scummer* by John Wayne Comunale
#038__*Cockblock* by C.V. Hunt
#037__*Irrationalia* by Andersen Prunty
#036__*Full Brutal* by Kristopher Triana
#035__*Office Mutant* by Pete Risley
#034__*Death Pacts and Left-Hand Paths* by John Wayne Comunale
#033__*Home Is Where the Horror Is* by C.V. Hunt
#032__*This Town Needs A Monster* by Andersen Prunty
#031__*The Fetishists* by A.S. Coomer
#030__*Ritualistic Human Sacrifice* by C.V. Hunt
#029__*The Atrocity Vendor* by Nick Cato
#028__*Burn Down the House and Everyone In It* by Zachary T. Owen

#027__*Misery and Death and Everything Depressing* by C.V. Hunt
#026__*Naked Friends* by Justin Grimbol
#025__*Ghost Chant* by Gina Ranalli
#024__*Hearers of the Constant Hum* by William Pauley III
#023__*Hell's Waiting Room* by C.V. Hunt
#022__*Creep House: Horror Stories* by Andersen Prunty
#021__*Other People's Shit* by C.V. Hunt
#020__*The Party Lords* by Justin Grimbol
#019__*Sociopaths In Love* by Andersen Prunty
#018__*The Last Porno Theater* by Nick Cato
#017__*Zombieville* by C.V. Hunt
#016__*Samurai Vs. Robo-Dick* by Steve Lowe
#015__*The Warm Glow of Happy Homes* by Andersen Prunty
#014__*How To Kill Yourself* by C.V. Hunt
#013__*Bury the Children in the Yard: Horror Stories* by Andersen Prunty
#012__*Return to Devil Town (Vampires in Devil Town Book Three)* by Wayne Hixon
#011__*Pray You Die Alone: Horror Stories* by Andersen Prunty
#010__*King of the Perverts* by Steve Lowe
#009__*Sunruined: Horror Stories* by Andersen Prunty
#008__*Bright Black Moon (Vampires in Devil Town Book Two)* by Wayne Hixon
#007__*Hi I'm a Social Disease: Horror Stories* by Andersen Prunty
#006__*A Life On Fire* by Chris Bowsman
#005__*The Sorrow King* by Andersen Prunty
#004__*The Brothers Crunk* by William Pauley III
#003__*The Horribles* by Nathaniel Lambert
#002__*Vampires in Devil Town* by Wayne Hixon
#001__*House of Fallen Trees* by Gina Ranalli
#000__*Morning is Dead* by Andersen Prunty

www.ingramcontent.com/pod-product-compliance
Lightning Source LLC
La Vergne TN
LVHW030922080826
845145LV00013B/3009

* 9 7 8 1 9 5 7 5 0 4 1 5 5 *